LUCIFER:

THE INTERVIEW

BY

JAMES GREEN

James Green

This novel is a work of fiction. Names, characters, places, and incidents either are the product of the author's imagination or are used fictitiously, and any resemblance to actual persons, living or dead, businesses, companies, events, or locales is entirely coincidental.

Library of Congress Cataloging-in-Publication Data

Lucifer The Interview/James Green

ISBN978-0-9850020-3-9

Front and Back Cover Design by The Intelligent Consulting Design Team

www.intelligentpublishing.org

James Green

James Green

James Green

James Green

THE PREFACE

This is the story of a young man, Christian L. Smith. His experience with Satan is an up close, personal and sometimes horrific one. His lifelong encounters and experiences are like none ever told before.

Millions of people confess to believe in God. Do they say it out of faith? Out of tradition? How many of those people believe in a tangible devil? All those questions intrigue Christian as he decides to find out on his own what is real, and what is the truth.

This is a story of love, hate, jealousy, murder, deception, and truth. When you are lucky enough to be faced with the absolute truth, would you be ready for it? Sooner or later everyone has to choose, and you'll see what choice Christian L. Smith is forced to make once he is face to face...

...with The Devil himself.

James Green

THE INTRODUCTION

For a year now I've had this obsession, I guess you can call it. This obsession has cost me my girlfriend, my best friend's life and even my sanity. My name is Christian L. Smith born October 31st 1986. My name appears to be normal to the average person, unless we met, got to know each other or you happen to ask me what my middle name was. My middle name is Lucifer. I didn't get the chance to ask my parents why they named me that. They died when I was a small child. In fact, I didn't know where the name even came from until a year ago. Previous to that I would receive blank looks or stares until it became normal to me. I was the kind of kid other kids would've loved to tease or bully, but that never happened to me. On the other hand I didn't have too many friends either. It seemed if everyone was afraid to talk to me or even be near me. I wouldn't say I dressed Gothic, but I did have an affinity for black. Black shirts, black pants, black socks, black shoes, even a black book bag. I always smelled nice, had good hygiene, my hair was always groomed. I've always looked handsome if I may say so myself. The one thing different about me, that no one knew was that I've always had a presence with me. You know the feeling you get when you're in a room alone and you get that shiver when someone enters the room; well mine was much more than that. I could actually see the presence! It didn't talk, didn't move, it only appeared and

James Green

disappeared. I felt the presence all the time, but I could only see it at night. In the beginning when I saw the figure I felt the deepest, darkest fear one could imagine. Eventually I got used to it and began to expect its arrival every night.

James Green

THE BEGINNING

When I was three years old my parents died in a house fire. I remember being carried out by one of the firemen; he got me out of the burning blaze without a scratch. When they carried me out I wasn't coughing or anything. I stood next to the man that saved my life as we watched the rest of the fireman take out the fire. He held my hand the whole time until the ambulance got there. I remember looking up at him seeing his big mustache and a smile on his face. "It'll be ok son" I remember him saying. I didn't know anything about fire, or death then. I figured I'd see my mom and dad again when it was all over. No one ever figured out why the fire got started.

I had a few photographic memories of my parents. None of them seem to be happy memories. Only blank stares and my mom looking at me with tears in her eyes. I always remember the running mascara. They didn't talk much and I couldn't remember them even smiling. I do remember the ride in the ambulance on the way to the hospital though. All the paramedics were rushing around in a panic; I imagine it was because I was just a young child. When I woke up lying in the hospital bed with some kind of mask on, I recall seeing the presence for the first time in the corner of my room. When I first looked

James Green

up, I thought it was my dad. I couldn't tell who it was, so I became terrified! The figure didn't say anything, it just stood there motionless.

The next day a few people dressed in suits came in talking to each other. They would look at me then smile before going back to talking to one another. The only time anyone came in was when they were bringing me something to eat.

That night I was awakened by a small gust of wind. I opened my eyes and saw that the presence had returned. I didn't see anyone outside of my room window, with the mask on my face screaming seemed pointless. . . even for a three year old. I pulled the cover over my head as any other kid would do in that situation, until I fell asleep.

James Green

THE ORPHANAGE

The next morning I was taken to a house that I soon learned to be an orphanage. When I got to my room, I realized I wasn't going to see my parents again.

I lived in an orphanage the rest of my childhood and years to come. They allowed me to go to public school; they said I was a smart kid. I was a straight "A" student. I would always bring home awards from school. Some of the other kids didn't go to school and were not fond of my accomplishments. No one said anything to me but I would hear them talking about me sometimes. They would call me a nerd or a loser or any harsh insult that they could think of. One day a kid finally decided he had enough of my awards and blocked me from getting into my room. "What you got there nerd boy, another award" he said in a mocking voice. "Um, yea, want to see?" I said. He took my award, looked at his friends across the hall and ripped it. I remember the rage I had built in me. I wasn't scared but I didn't want to fight either. He threw the ripped pieces and walked back towards his friends laughing. I walked back in my room angry and hurt. I started to form tears when I felt a familiar gust of wind enter the room. I didn't see anything but it gave me comfort. A few days later when returning home from school I saw a missing child poster in the hallway. It was a picture of the kid that ripped my award. I never saw him again.

James Green

THE BIBLE

Growing up I always liked to read, I would read an entire book in one day, no matter how big it was. I would read a book once and be done with it. I would remember whatever I needed to remember and that would be good enough. But one book caught my particular interest unlike any other book...The Holy Bible. I was always confused about why were there so many religions and beliefs, so many different Gods people worshiped, and why when it came down to it, no one really wanted to talk about it. I mean you could get a short surface cliché conversation, but when it came down to talking about religion, people always avoided it. I think that was part of the reason why I became more interested. I mean from page one it contradicted everything I was learning in school; how the universe came to be, how people came to be. It was such a toss up, who was telling the truth? If this book was wrong from page one what was the point of believing anything this book had to say.

I started reading The Holy Bible my senior year in high school. I'd read it during study hall, during lunch, sometimes I'd sneak and read it in class when I felt I had no reason to listen to the teacher at the time. My English teacher, Ms. Kirkpatrick, caught me reading it one day because I finished my test early. She picked it up, looked at it, looked at me, handed it back closed and said "There's no time for that right

James Green

now, take out your English book. An education should be your number one priority." In history class any question I had about God would be avoided and treated as the subject were some fictional fantasy. The strangest thing to me was that when I read the book at home, the presence would always disappear. Although it's presence gave me a peaceful feeling, it also made me feel sort of uncomfortable.

Many times I tried to speak to the presence. I didn't know what to say outside of "Who are you", "Why are you here" or "Is there anything you want from me." It never answered me though, therefore I would give it a hello when it entered or a goodbye when I felt it leave.

As I read more and more of The Holy Bible I came across a character. A character named Lucifer. I always thought my middle name was made up so I really got excited when I saw the name in The Holy Bible! Lucifer was the anointed cherub. I had no idea what that meant so I had to look it up. It means he was set apart for God's divine purpose, "bestowal of God's divine favor." God had given Lucifer authority and power in Heaven. He made him perfect; he was the most beautiful and enchanted angel in Heaven. After reading that small passage, it provided an instant shot of gratification to my existence. It also gave me a new found appreciation for my parents. They thought enough of me to name me after a beautiful and powerful angel in Heaven

James Green

THE ENCOUNTER

Back at school to my surprise I got a lot of female attention. It was more so a lot of smiles, looks with batting eyelashes and some had the courage to speak. A kid of my status getting even a little attention like that didn't sit too well with the captain of the football team Brad Manning. Ever since he became the starting quarterback in the tenth grade he felt he was king of Lockwood High. I would always see him staring at me in the hallway with an "I'm going to kick your ass" look on his eyes. Sometimes he'd brush against me when we walked by each other, nothing too hard to grab my attention though. But one day he was talking to his girlfriend after class, the captain of the cheerleading team Amy Hunter. I was walking out of my history class headed to my locker when Amy and I caught eyes. The immediate chemistry of our stare made me forget where I was going. Seems she felt the same way because it was at least 20 seconds of Brad talking and her not listening or even looking at him. He followed her eyes and they led right to me. If I wasn't mesmerizided with Amy's eyes, I would've seen Brad walk over and punch the living daylights out of me. He hit me so hard my head hit the lockers before I fell to the ground. If I wasn't unconscious at the time I bet it would've hurt a lot worse when it happened. When I finally woke up the hallway was empty, no students, no teachers, not anyone. I suddenly got the hugest headache; I could barely open my

James Green

eyes. As I went to stand up I felt someone helping me up. When I turned around to thank whoever it was; there was no one there. I had always felt the presence but it never touched me before. I walked to the bathroom to straighten myself up. When I looked in the mirror the whole right side of my face was completely swollen and on top of that it was completely sore! I could feel my blood pressure rising with the inclined rush of rage, I wanted revenge. If he made my face look like this then his will have to look ten times worse! My heart was pounding, my hands were sweating, and my eyes were watering. I washed my face and got myself together. As I was leaving the bathroom I felt a hand rest on my shoulder. It was for a couple seconds then it left. I don't know what it was for but it gave me comfort at the time. I finished out the rest of the school day. I was still mad but I had calmed down from earlier. If anyone said anything to me I didn't know, I was focused on what I was going to do to Brad when I saw him again. I forgot I had to stay late that day to finish up a project I had in science class. The teacher wanted to display my project in the upcoming science fair. When I was done, I went to get my jacket out of my locker. The hallway felt bitterly cold and creepy as I was walking down it. I got the feeling of déjà vu but I had no idea what it was. I paid it no mind and proceeded to put my jacket on. An old brown torn piece of paper fell out of my locker. I thought it was a piece of brown paper bag but when I felt it, it was more like a cloth. On the front of it was some writing in fine red ink. It was too thick to be from an ink pen and too

James Green

thin to be from a paint brush. The words read "*FOR YOU.*" I looked around to ensure this wasn't some kind of joke. Normally I would've thrown it away but I put it in my pocket and walked home. On the way home it got a little windy, so I zipped up my jacket. When I looked down I saw another piece of paper that resembled the one I had in my pocket. I couldn't see any writing on it, so I went to pick it up. I failed in my attempt because the wind blew the paper, it didn't blow it completely away though, just enough for me to follow it. I didn't keep reaching for it because I didn't want to look like a weirdo in the street chasing a piece of paper. Instead I followed behind it... like a weirdo. I became so intrigued by where the paper was going by the time I looked up I didn't know where I was. "Well I came this far" I said to myself and continued to follow the paper. It led me to some woods I'd never been in, let alone seen before. I don't wonder around the neighborhood, too much so neighborhood wasn't familiar. I followed the paper down the main trail for a minute then it blew off the trail. I was reluctant to follow it but I figured since I had come this far I might as well keep going. I heard a few flies and I began to get uncomfortable, I hate bugs let alone walking through woods! Since no one was around I finally decided to try to pick up the paper. It blew one more hard time before coming to a final rest. As I picked it up I felt a few rain drops on my head. Now I'm feeling like a moron and angry because I'm lost from chasing a piece of paper and I'm about to get rained on. I looked up to see how dark the clouds were, maybe I had

James Green

time to find my way home before the rain came down...and what I saw, made me vomit.

I saw Brad hanging from a tree. He was naked and lifeless. What I thought was rain on my head turned out to be his blood. I had no idea what to think. I was panicked, I was scared. I was so freaked out I began to cry. I backed up to take a last look at him and saw something carved in his chest. It was hard to make out with all the tears in my eyes. I wiped my eyes and saw that it was a pentagram. It looked like those stars we drew in preschool with all the lines in them. On his stomach there were some words carved. . . "FOR YOU." I quickly reached for the paper in my pocket to make sure that's what I read earlier. This couldn't be real, who would do such a heinous act? I didn't even have friends close enough to avenge a punch in the face for me. Brad had to be at least 14-15 feet in the air, how did he even get up there? The tree didn't look anywhere near climbable. And now this guy's blood is on my forehead and shirt. What if the police think I did it? There are at least 20 kids that saw me get punched in the face earlier. I thought about calling the police or telling someone living nearby. Instead I ran and found my way home. I sat in my bed shaking. I remembered the blood, so I ran to the bathroom to wash it off. I cried again as I washed my face and threw away my shirt. I gazed into the mirror for a brief second. Something in me told me to cut the lights off. I cut them off, turned around and saw the presence standing by the window. My whole life he was always a black blur when he appeared;

James Green

but now he was more defined. I could see the shape of a head and what appeared to be a silhouette of unspread wings. I couldn't see any eyes but it felt like we stared at each other for an eternity. "Did you do this?" It stood there for a second before disappearing into thin air.

James Green

THE OBSESSION BEGINS

About a week later, I was on my way to school (*I was about an hour late because I overslept*). Ever since seeing Brad in those woods I wasn't the same. When I got to school I saw everyone in the hallway hugged together and crying. I knew what the reason was but I acted as if I didn't know what was going on. I saw some of the football team wearing Brad's number painted on their faces. On the graffiti wall it read "RIP BRAD, WE MISS YOU." I saw Amy crying on the shoulder of her best friend Michelle. I was always antisocial but all I could think about was when we locked eyes a week before. I walked up to her slowly and placed my hand on her shoulder. "Are you ok?" I asked. She looked up and hugged me as if she were waiting on me all morning. She cried on my shoulder, didn't say anything, just cried. I knew she was sad but for my own selfish reasons, I was happy. I was hoping I wasn't smiling at the time; I didn't want to seem inappropriate with everything going on. After a few minutes I pushed her away softly, still holding on to her arms, I looked her in her eyes and said "If you ever need anyone to talk to. . . " She nodded and said "Thank you." That day it seemed teachers didn't want to teach too much of anything. It was a real sad environment. In every class the teachers all mumbled, "Take out your books and read please. " The principal talked over the PA system during every class requesting a moment of silence so we

James Green

could all take the time and remember Brad. My last memory of Brad now was him punching me in the face and then hanging from a tree. I decided to get back to reading my Bible. It was the only book I had been reading over the last couple of weeks. I wanted to know more about Lucifer. I wanted to know more about the angel who bared the same name as I did. The book was so huge; I didn't know where to look. I took my cell phone out my pocket and Google searched his name. As I looked at the search results, I became more and more disturbed. "Father of lies," "the devil," and all the horrible images I saw. I didn't feel proud of my name anymore. Why would my parents name me that? I clicked on images, my curiosity and disgust began taking over. Out of all the pictures that disturbed me, one really made my stomach turn! I saw the upside down pentagram that was carved on Brad's chest. I searched "inverted pentagram." It represented the dark side and it was a pagan symbol. It was a symbol used by "Satanists." What was Satanism anyway?

This is when my obsession began. I had to know more. It became more than knowing about The Holy Bible now. I wanted to know about Lucifer. Why was he evil? Has this been him in my presence my whole life? If so, why me? I looked up videos on YouTube searching for Satan, Lucifer or the devil, trying to learn more. It became compulsive, the urge I had to read The Holy Bible turned into me learning about Lucifer. I feel the biggest mistake in all my research

James Green

happened when I found the book I thought would tell me all I needed to know. I bought a copy of "Satan's Bibel."

The first day I opened the book at home I felt the presence like never before. It was more intense than when he helped me up, or when he touched my shoulder. He appeared as a broad solid matter now instead of a cloudy blur. Everything was still black, I could see the wings more clearly, and I could see the outline of hair. . Its hair looked like mine from the outline. The figure was about 6 foot 6 about six inches taller than me. Even though everything was black, I could tell it had on some sort of a breastplate. There was an instant fear that came over me. I don't know why I was scared. He had been right there my whole life, why was I so afraid now? I didn't know what to do so I began to read the book I bought; I thought that maybe reading would calm my nerves. As I turned to the first page, the figure took a step forward. My teeth started to chatter. As scared as I was, I was still curious. I turned another page; I turned it without even reading. He took another step. A familiar gust of wind came through my room. I turned another page and he took another step. I turned the pages until he stood three inches from my chair. I could feel him breathing on my forehead. I was so frightened that my hands couldn't turn another page. Once the presence realized I wasn't going to turn another page, he began to spread his wings. Even though there was no color, they were beautiful wings. They spread with such grace giving me a slight comfort but then the horrific image of the goat's head suddenly flew

James Green

towards my face until it almost touched me "*READ!*" it screamed. Suddenly another gush of wind blew and I was in the room alone. The presence was gone; all I had was this book. All comfort I ever had with the presence was now out the window. I was now petrified that it may return. I stared at the book with tears in my eyes. However, I knew I was still going to read it . I knew it just like a cigarette smoker knows they're going to finish the pack.

James Green

THE NEW GIRLFRIEND

The next day in school, I ran into Amy after science class. Looking at her took all my stress away; I didn't think about the book, I didn't think about Brad, I didn't think about anything. I forgot about being anti-social, I forgot about all the negative things that would now cross my mind every second. I gathered up all the courage I could muster up and I asked her out on a date. She told me she wanted to go see a scary movie. To be honest, I thought she suggested that because she thought I would enjoy it. How I dressed, my demeanor could generate the perception that I was a scary movie fanatic. "I love scary movies," I said with a smile. I was lying though; I had actually never been to the movies because I didn't have that many friends during my lifetime.

Our dates started off once a week on the weekends, before escalating to two or three times a week. As good as a time I was having with her, I had a growing desire of getting back to my book. I don't know why I was so eager to get back to it. Although every encounter increased the fear I had, I continued to read. I read the book so much, but I was never satisfied. "I craved more." I started to look up books about Satanism. I never practiced anything I read, I was always just curious as to why. The things that I read were so confusing to me. In one way, I could relate to what I read and the next paragraph would make

James Green

me sick to my stomach. I didn't want to borrow books from the library because I didn't want everyone to know what I was reading so I continued to buy the books. One problem was that I didn't have a lot of money.

I picked up a job at the local super market to fund my obsession. I had a lot on my plate now, my job, school, my obsession, and my new girlfriend Amy. Our dates turned into visits. It didn't start off sexual; we usually rented a movie, did some homework together or just cuddled and laughed.

One Friday night after watching *A Nightmare on Elm Street*, we were laying in my bed cuddling, she held me as if she were still scared from the movie. I felt so at peace being by her side. She slowly looked up at me, we locked eyes, we moved in slower and slower to engage in a beautiful kiss. . We both inhaled as if the kiss cured some kind of hunger. That was actually our first kiss, our first real passionate kiss. As I went in for another, I got a sudden feeling of déjà vu. I felt a familiar gust of wind. I looked around hoping I didn't see the presence in my room. I looked towards the corner of the room, I looked towards the door, and I even looked behind me. "What's wrong honey?" Amy said. As I turned around to tell her that nothing was the problem, I saw the presence behind her. All I could do is stare and shiver because of the sudden fear that came upon me. The presence never appeared while I was with someone else. "What is it?" Amy said with a scared

tone in her voice. She looked in my eyes but I wasn't looking back. She turned around to see what I was looking at and the presence vanished. She turned back around. "That movie really got to you huh" she giggled. "Yeah" I responded back trying to giggle, the fear I still had made the giggle obviously fake.

James Green

THE GREETING

The next morning there was a knock at my door. I turned around to see if Amy was still there, I ended up falling asleep before I got to tell her goodbye. She left a note on the pillow, and before I could read it there was a knock on my door again. I had forgotten all about the first knock and quickly opened the door and it was my neighbor; well the kid that stayed in the room next door.

"Hey...um Mark" he held his hand out for me to shake it.

I looked down at his hand as If I didn't know what to do. All this time we've lived under the same roof and this was his first time speaking to me. I was a little surprised but excited at the same time.

"Christian" I said as I finally shook his hand. "So what can I do for you?" I asked.

He told me that he wanted to meet me since we have lived next door to each other practically forever.

"I always mean to speak to you, but every time I see you there's this kind of creepiness, like you're sad about something. I always say I'll wait until the next time I see him, maybe he'll look like he's in a better mood to meet someone," he laughed. "But yesterday I saw you

James Green

with a girl and you were finally smiling. I didn't want to interrupt so I figured I would wait until now...so here I am!"

I invited him in. He seemed amazed at the things I had in my room. Everything I had was new now that I had a job. Everything was new...new and black. He sat on my chair as I sat on my bed.

"I...I have to be honest with you" he said. . "I also wanted to know, well. . . I hear you talking all the time through the wall and I don't hear anyone talking back.. I hear you say hello and good bye but I never hear anyone come or go".

I told him he must have been talking about my girlfriend, when I speak to her.

"No no...I have been hearing you for some time now, I was just curious," he said.

I knew what he was referring to but I responded, "I don't know, maybe it was my TV or something."

He had a look that said he knew I wasn't being completely honest.

"Forget I asked," he said. "Anyway, do you want to hang out one day or something? We can go to the mall, eat or hang out at the malt shop." *Wow, my first friend,* I thought.

James Green

"Sure man," I responded. "Cool, well I guess I'll see you around then" he smiled and went back to his room.

James Green

THE NIGHTMARE

I reached for the note Amy left on my pillow. *"Sorry I didn't wake you before I left, you were fast asleep and I didn't want to wake you. Love, Amy xoxo."* That was the first time someone used the word love and involved me. I must admit it put a really big smile on my face. I reached to put the note with the picture I had of Amy and I, we had taken a picture while walking down the street one day. When I put the note down, I noticed something wrong with the picture. Amy's face had been burned out. The picture didn't smell burnt and I couldn't imagine who would come in my room and do something so random. All I could think of is what happened to Brad so I panicked and quickly grabbed the phone to call Amy. She picked up.

"Hello"... "Hello, hello, are you ok?" I asked in a panicked voice.

She laughed, "Yes honey, why wouldn't I be? You're not still creeped out by that movie are you?"

"Yeah, yeah I must be" I responded and hung up without saying good-bye. I was so relieved I forgot my manners. I decided to take a short nap before getting back to my book. Deep down I was scared not to read because I thought the presence would be upset with me.

James Green

About an hour later, I woke up in a cold sweat and deep breathing. I had a terrible nightmare. I was three years old; I woke up from the smell of smoke and a gust of wind that gave me the chills. I got up and opened my bedroom door. I saw everything burning and my mom screaming my name and crying. I saw my dad running out the door but for some reason I couldn't get a good look at him. I turned back to my mom and took a step. Before I could take another, the floor caved in where she was and she fell to the first floor along with the rest of the burning matter. As I went to run down the stairs, someone picked me up and attempted to rush me outside. It must have been a fireman because I could feel his hard helmet hitting against my head. When we got outside, I stood next to him and held his hand as the rest of the firefighters attempted to put the fire out. I looked up to see who the man was that saved my life and all I saw was the face of a goat "READ!" it screamed. I let out a horrific scream then I woke up. My heart was pounding and I could barely catch my breath.

James Green

THE "ACCIDENT"

When I calmed down, I picked up the book to begin reading. I saw words but I wasn't really reading. All I could think of was my mom and watching her die. I only knew her for three years and forgot most memories of her but I felt like I missed her. I wanted to know what happened. I wanted to know about my dad. Who was he, what did he look like, did he look like me, and why didn't he help us?

I realized I was almost late for work so I hurried up and got dressed. I made it just in the nick of time, time enough to clock in and go straight to the back and begin getting merchandise to stock the shelves. The manager didn't see me, I liked to keep it that way; I wasn't too comfortable with the idea of authority, someone telling me what to do and how to do it. I began putting the cereal on the shelves. It seemed like it was a million boxes. As I put up the sixth box, I noticed something strange. The store was entirely too quiet. I looked around and saw there were no customers, no employees, just eeriness. I walked down the aisle I was in towards the front of the store. Before I could reach the end, someone tapped me on the shoulder. It was an old lady...

"Excuse me, can you tell me where my daughter is?"

"What?" I asked with a confused face.

James Green

She repeated, "Can you tell me where my daughter is, I can't find her."

I really didn't know what to do, so I grabbed her by the hand and started walking her to the front of the store. "Did you lose her in here?" I asked.

"No" she said. "She died in a house fire in 1985...AND YOU'RE NEXT!"

I turned around and she had the head of a goat. I let go of her hand and ran as fast as I could out the store. I could hear her creepy laugh as I was running away. What was happening to me? Ever since I got punched in the face, my life seemed to be going down the drain. The only thing I had to be happy about was Amy. I started daydreaming about her smile as I was running home to make myself feel better. I got so deep in thought I didn't see that I ran in the street. I heard the loud horn of a Honda Civic as it hit me. I rolled on top of the hood but before I rolled over the whole car, I was picked up and placed gently on the ground. The person that was driving slammed on the brakes and his car quickly stopped. He got out the car and ran towards me.

"Hey! Asshole!" he said in an angry voice.

It was a middle-aged guy that was bald at the top with hair on the sides of his head.

James Green

"What were you thinking huh?!" he screamed.

"I'm ok" I responded. He gave me a hard push before he walked away back to his car. "Be more fucking careful next time...dumbass."

I was still in shock from being hit by a car and the landing I was barley paying him attention. As I slowly turned to start walking home, there was a big explosion. BOOM! I turned around and the Honda Civic was in flames...and so was the rude middle-aged man. I panicked and ran home as fast as I could. When I got there, I ran up the stairs. Mark was on his way down the stairs, but I had to get to my room, so I had no time for small talk.

"Hey! Christian?" he said trying to get my attention.

I slammed myself in my chair with my face in my hands. There was so much confusion, so much fear. I attempted to think of Amy but the last time I tried that I got hit by a car.

"Hey. . . You okay dude?"

I looked up and it was Mark standing in my doorway. I shook my head attempting to say words but I couldn't gather any to say.

He placed his hand on my shoulder as he sat on the bed.

"What's your story?" he asked.

James Green

At first, I thought I should feel annoyed by his question but it was comforting that someone cared to ask me. I took a deep breath, looked up and we began...well I began to tell him my story. I told him about the fire, the inkling amount I knew about my father, which consisted of him always walking out. I told him about the few images I had of my mom. I told him everything as if I were telling a psychologist. I did omit a major factor though. I didn't dare tell him about the presence I had with me. Really didn't want to lose the only friend I had that quickly. He seemed interested in what I was saying. The look that he gave me was as if he knew there was more, but I wasn't going to spill it.

"I know a lady," he said with a small smirk on his face, "well I know of a lady, I hear she can talk to spirits...you know dead people."

"Dead people?" I asked.

"Yea...you know, maybe she can contact your mom," he said.

As crazy as it sounded, I was intrigued. The first thing I thought was how the hell was this woman able to do that in the first place, but that thought soon escaped my curiosity.

"Ok" I said.

"Ok man...I'll see what I can do," he said as he got up and left the room.

James Green

THE CLUE

When he closed the door, I noticed some strange writing on the back of it. "LOSE HER" was written on the door in what appeared to red paint. It looked more like blood; I walked up to get a closer look. I rubbed my finger through one of the drips coming down from the letters. I could tell it was blood on my finger, it looked like the blood I had on my forehead when I found Brad. A small gust of wind entered the room. I turned around expecting to see the presence but it wasn't there. I noticed my book was blown open. I picked it up to read it as I sat. I saw a light coming from my nightstand where I kept my Bible. I opened it to see The Holy Bible on top everything...it was on top of my pictures, some random papers I had in there and my letter from Amy. I couldn't remember if I had placed it on top of everything like that but I closed the drawer and went back to reading the Satanic Bibel. The title of the chapter that was showing was called SACRIFICE. It went into grave detail about sacrificing animals, and small children and young women. It also talked about the benefits of what you would receive if you participated in such acts. I was disturbed by it but I was also confused as to why there would be reward for such terrible acts...crimes at that.

"Christian," I looked up quickly to see where the voice was coming from...I saw nothing.

James Green

I opened the closet door, looked under the bed; why I looked under there I have no idea. As I stood, the presence was directly in front of me. I was so startled I fell back in my chair.

"Christian," he said in a calm manner. I was for sure it was a man now by the sound of his voice. "Christian," he repeated again.

"Yes," I said as my teeth slightly chattered.

He let out the deepest loudest voice, nothing like how he just sounded a second ago... "LOSE HER!" he screamed as flew out the window. I figured it was about time I stopped being naïve and realize that he was the one that murdered Brad; that he was the one that burned the picture of Amy, and he was the one that wrote on my door with that blood that came from who knows where, and he was the one who murdered that man in the street. Could he have had something to do with that missing kid all those years ago? If he was protecting me all those times why would he want me to get rid of my girlfriend, Amy was the best thing I had in my life at the moment. I was grateful for being protected but by no means did I want anyone to be murdered and I definitely wasn't going to dump my girlfriend. Not for him, not for anyone! On the other hand, what would he do to me if I didn't listen?

James Green

THE APPOINTMENT IS SET

About a week went by and everything was going normal, well at least as normal as I was used to. I would read and the presence would stand in the corner, as if he were pleased. I tried my hardest to avoid Amy until I figured things out. I would tell her I was busy with work, or school, or that I was hanging with Mark.

On Saturday morning I was awaken by my cell phone ringing. I looked all over the bed, I checked my pockets, I checked my dirty clothes but I couldn't find my phone. I stood still so I could follow the sound of the ring. The ring led me to my nightstand. I opened the drawer and my phone was sitting on top of The Holy Bible. It was Amy calling. How did my phone get in there anyway? I never put the phone in my nightstand. Before I could pick up the phone it went to voicemail. As I was pushing the call back button Amy called again. I was happy it was her but I was nervous about her asking to see me.

"Christian." I could tell she was crying by the sound of her voice. "What's wrong?" I asked.

"What's going on with you? Why does it seem like things are different between us? Did I do something wrong?"

James Green

It hurt my heart to hear her voice knowing it was my entire fault. I was scared, I didn't want to give her up but I didn't want to risk losing her.

"I just have a lot going on," I said.

"WELL TELL ME!" she screamed.

I didn't know what to say so I started to tell her about my parents and the fire in 1989, about the fireman, about the paramedics and how I ended up in an orphanage. I left out the part about the encounter I had in the hospital. I didn't know what she would think of me if I brought something like that up. She asked me a few questions about my parents but I didn't have too much to respond with, all I could tell her was about how I pictured my mom and how I pictured my dad.

"Amy," I said before she could get another question out, "Do you believe in the devil?" I guess the question threw her off a little.

"Like the devil, the guy with the red horns and pitch fork?"

"I guess," I responded. "I mean, I never really thought about it I guess," she said.

I took a deep breath; I finally decided I would tell her about the presence. If I loved her like I said I did and she loved me then eventually she would have to accept the biggest secret I have had my entire life.

James Green

"I have to tell you something Amy."

"Yes." she said.

"I..."

"Christian! Christian!" Mark burst in my room before I could say anything. "I got good news buddy!"

"Christian? What is it?" Amy said.

I couldn't tell her now so I said I would call her back later on. She sounded hurt and disappointed but she hung up without a fight.

"Well," he said, "remember I told you about the woman that could talk to dead people, well I got us a meeting!"

He seemed real excited; I wondered did he have anyone he wanted to talk to from the dead. I know I had a million questions for my mom. As willing as I was, I was still nervous. It's not like talking to dead people is a common every day adventure for someone.

"So when's the meeting?" I asked. He had a funny look on his face before he responded.

"In about four hours."

"Four hours!" I screamed. I suddenly realized I had nothing else to do, so I just said ok.

James Green

The place was at a woman's house. Madam Vodsky was her name. Her house was about a 30-minute walk away. As we walked, we laughed, joked and talked about normal things. I missed Amy but it was nice talking to another guy, even though we weren't talking about much.

"Man, that is one big ass bird," he said.

I looked up and saw a flock of black birds flying the same way we were walking.

"Which one?" I asked. He pointed to the one in front.

"That's no bird," I whispered to myself. I never saw the presence in the daylight but I had seen him enough times to know what he would look like. The huge beautiful wings looked all too familiar. I was terrified but I didn't want Mark to know anything.

"What?" he said.

"Yeah...yeah that is a big bird," I said with an uncomfortable smirk on my face.

The flock of birds seemed to lead us to the house. When we finally got to Madam Vodsky's development, the birds had flown away. The houses were huge and beautiful, nothing like they were when I was at the orphanage.

James Green

THE SE'ANCE

When we got to her house, we stood there on the porch starring at each other. I guess he was as creeped out as I was now. We gave each other a nod and the door opened before I got the chance to knock. There was no one at the door to greet us. It seemed too much like a scary movie.

"Let's get out of here," I turned and said to Mark.

Mark agreed but as we turned around, we heard a pleasant voice with what sounded like a German accent.

"Mark, Christian, so glad you could make it."

It was a lady in her mid-30's. She was beautiful; she wore a scarf around her head like a fortuneteller I had seen on TV before.

"Come, come we have much to do," she said as she led us to the basement.

When we reached the basement to my surprise, there were other people waiting. There were five waiting tables placed around the main table where Madam Vodsky did her work. Each table had a game in the middle. One table had dominoes, the next table had dice, the next an Ouija board, another one had Chess, and the fifth one had

James Green

Mexican bingo. There were two seats for Mark and I at the bingo table, so we took a seat. All the games seemed so random, but I guess they were there for entertainment or to occupy your time as you waited your turn. There were candles lit throughout the entire basement, so no incandescent light was needed. One wall had pictures of beautiful creatures that appeared to be angels. I had never seen them before but they were all beautiful. The ceiling was painted like a night sky. There were stars everywhere, which made up certain patterns like different animals. There was a sun in the middle right above the main table, which was a bit confusing since I thought it was supposed to be a night sky I was looking at.

When it was time to get started, Madam Vodsky stood at her seat.

"Everyone…it is time we begin, you will all be helped in the order you came. First up, may I see Ms. Laura Hamilton." A woman got up from the table that had the Chess board.

She walked over to the main table and sat directly across from Madam Vodsky. "What is it that I may do for you my dear?" Madam Vodsky said with a smile.

Ms. Laura looked around the room for a second; it seemed she was a little scared. "I want to speak to my dead grandmother," she said. Madam Vodsky closed her eyes for about 20 seconds. Suddenly

James Green

you could see her eyes start rolling behind her eyelids. She started convulsing, I didn't know whether to see if she was ok or not. As I started to get up to see what was wrong her eyes opened.

"Your grandmother says she would love to speak to you Laura...are you ready?" When Laura replied "yes," there was a familiar small gust of wind that entered the room. All the candles blew out except the ones that surrounded the main table. Madam Vodsky closed her eyes again, looked down "She is ready." I heard her say. I turned around to look at Mark; he seemed paralyzed with fear.

"Hey, you ok? You don't believe any of this do you?" I said with a smile. He slowly lifted his hand pointing at the wall across from the main table. I looked over and there was a light slowly coming through the wall.

"Laura...Laura, this is your grandmother." The voice was coming from the light. Laura was so terrified she didn't utter a word. Then the light finally came through the wall, we could all see the image of an old woman.

"WOW! Mark, do you see the..." before I could finish my sentence Mark was already running out the door. There was no way I was going to be alone down there so I ran after him. I kept calling his name as I was chasing after him down the street. I don't know if it was the fear or Mark was really that fast. It took about a minute for me to

catch up with him. We stopped running for a second, we were both out of breath.

"Christian," it was hard for him to get his words out he was so out of breath, "dude I'm sorry, I didn't know it was going to be like that, I thought it was going to be, some creepy old lady that read some cards to us and we paid her a dollar or something, what the hell was that we just saw?"

I looked down at the ground with my hands on my knees. "I don't know," I said. As crazy as it was, I was still in amazement. I mean how was that possible? On our way walking back home, all I could think about is what went on when we left. What did the woman find out about her grandmother, what would have happened when I asked to speak to my mother, would all of my questions have been answered? I kept all my thoughts to myself, I didn't want to get Mark anymore worked up than he already was.

James Green

THE WARNING

A few days went by since the visit to Madam Vodsky's place. I could tell Mark was still terrified but he never said a word about it. The presence still came every night. I would read and he would stand in the corner, it became the norm again. I wondered if he forgot about Amy, I was so ready to see her. I decided to call her because I knew prom was coming up soon. I thought she would be mad at me from all the avoiding I was doing. To my surprise, she was happy to hear from me.

"Christian, I have something we need to talk about," she said over the phone.

I didn't let her finish because I was so excited to talk to her about prom.

"Just promise me one thing," she said. "Promise me we don't have to wear black."

I laughed out loud and agreed.

Back at school, you could tell everyone had prom on the brain. Everyone was discussing what to wear, what kind of car to drive, where after prom was going to be. I was walking down the hall after math

James Green

class looking for Amy. I bumped into a student that didn't look familiar. She had on a nice pair of eyeglasses, a white button up shirt and a pair of jeans on. She was very conservative.

"Excuse me, I'm sorry," I said trying to be polite.

"Hello Christian," she said. Before I could respond she said, "Are you interested in knowing the truth?"

I was so confused by now I had no idea what to say.

"Do you know who Jesus Christ is?" she asked.

I felt entirely too awkward by then so I just decided to slowly walk away.

"Don't give place to the devil Christian!" she hollered as I walked away.

No one in the hallway seemed to even notice her. The bell rang and the hallway got empty quickly. My encounter with the strange girl caused me to miss seeing Amy.

I finally caught up with Amy after school; we went to pick out a tux and a dress for prom. The employee was helpful at the store; she gave Amy a beautiful white dress to go try on in the dressing room. As she was changing, I began to ask the woman her opinion on what tux I

should try on. Before I could get a word out her smile turned to a serious almost possessed face.

"LOSE HER," she said, it almost sounded like a voice of a man.

"I'm sorry?" I replied.

"LOSE HER!" she said again.

Amy came from behind the dressing area as the woman's face quickly went back to the smiling face we saw when we walked in. I didn't want to startle Amy so I didn't say anything. After she picked her dress, we reserved it and quickly left. My mind was so out of it I didn't get the chance to pick a tux for myself. "You didn't get a tux," Amy said. I told her I didn't see anything I liked and would pick out one another day, maybe at a different place.

When we got back to my place, there was an envelope slid under my door.

"Who's that from?" Amy asked.

There was no return address on the envelope; it just said my name on the front in red ink. I was afraid to open it, but I did any way to keep Amy from being suspicions. When I opened it, it was an invitation. It had Mark's name on it in addition to mine. It was an invitation to meet with Madam Vodsky again; the date was set for Sunday. DON'T MISS it said at the bottom. If I didn't see those words, I

James Green

probably wouldn't have been so nervous. I quickly ran next door to show Mark the invitation.

"No way Dude, how did she even get our address?"

I wondered the same question myself. I knew I had to go back, there were too many questions I had, and why was the presence flying above us the first time we went. Was he leading me there? Was there something he wanted me to see? Although I feared him, it just seemed like I knew him for so long. When I walked back to my room, I saw Amy with a book in her hand. I ran and quickly snatched the book from her hand, no way was she going to know I read Satan's Bibel. To my surprise, it was The Holy Bible.

"I didn't know you read the Bible," she said.

"Um, yeah I started but I never finished, so...so you read The Holy Bible?" I asked.

"Well I actually just started since you asked me about the devil, I figure I might as well not go the rest of my life not knowing anything you know," she said with a smile.

"What made you look in my night stand?" I asked.

She told me the book wasn't in a drawer and that it was sitting on top of the nightstand. Now I know I wasn't crazy. That had to be the second or third time that book moved without me touching it. In

James Green

addition, where was my other book? I quickly thought. I got nervous and tried to look around without her noticing I was looking for something. I finally found it lying on the floor next to the bed. I gently slid it under the bed so she wouldn't accidently run into it. I really cut it close that time, I didn't know what she would've thought if she had seen that book and I really didn't want to see the presence's reaction if she saw it.

"Oh Christian, I almost forgot, I really have to talk to you about something," she said.

My mind was so exhausted I asked her could it wait. I could tell she didn't want to but she reluctantly agreed.

James Green

THE SÉANCE (part 2)

To my surprise that Sunday, I finally convinced Mark to go back to Madam Vodsky's house with me. There was no way I was going to miss this appointment. Who knows what would have happened if we did. Mark had no idea but I knew what the presence was capable of and I didn't want to take any chances. So we took the same path to get there. I could see the fear on Marks face. He barely spoke a word until about half way there.

"Hey, I meant to tell you I had Death tickets for next week, you want to go?"

Death was a popular rock band that happened to come from our city. It was their first time returning home since they became famous and started doing music videos and going on world tours.

"Hell yeah I want to go!" I responded.

The excitement over the band helped ease the fear the rest of the walk. The whole walk I kept looking at the sky to see if the "flock of birds" was following us this time. We actually didn't see them until we got to madam Vodsky's house. They were hovering over the house, all but one. There was one stooped down in the middle of the roof, it looked like it was watching us.

James Green

"Dude, what kind of bird is that? I mean I've seen huge birds, but I've never seen one that big, it almost looks like a person," Mark said.

"I don't know dude...maybe it's a huge vulture," I replied.

"Yeah, maybe" Mark said as we arrived to the front door.

As I reached to ring the doorbell, Mark just pushed the front door open. We looked at each other, simultaneously took a deep breath and headed toward the basement. I was feeling anxious, but Marks nervousness was making me nervous.

"Hello boys." Madam Vodsky met us at the bottom of the stairs. "I'm sorry I didn't come up and let you in but I was talking to the spirit and could not break contact, but I see you both found your way, good, please sit." We sat and waited again like the last time. This time we sat at the table with the Ouija board.

Mark whispered, "Dude, do you think these Ouija boards really work? I've seen them on TV but I always wondered if the people were faking you know."

I looked at the board, wasn't much to it, just some letters, numbers and a triangular looking piece with a magnifying glass in the middle.

"Only one way to find out," I replied.

James Green

We both put our hands on the piece and stared at each other.

"Dude, ask it a question," Mark said.

"I don't know what to ask it," I said as I looked around the room trying to come up with a question. There was a young woman across from us sitting at the table with the chessboard. She was a blond; she had on red high heels and a black mini skirt. She gave me a small grin when we caught eyes then she went back to playing chess. Madam Vodsky was at the main table lighting the rest of the candles. She took a seat, stared straight ahead, and then just closed her eyes. She didn't move, didn't make a noise, she just sat there.

"Dude, hurry up and ask it a question!" Mark said in a loud whisper.

"Um, dear Ouija board, please tell us something, um. . . important" I had no idea what to ask it, I'm not sure if that was even a question.

"What?" Mark said with a weird look on his face, "Dude what d..." before Mark could finish our hands started moving. The piece seemed to be moving over different letters.

"Dude you're moving it," Mark said with small laugh. I could tell by the way he said it; it wasn't him moving it either. I raised my head a little, to see what letters were hovering over. E,P,H,E,S,I, there

James Green

was a pen and paper on the table so I had to remember what the letters were so I could write them down when it was done. It kept going, A, N, S, four, two, and seven. When it stopped moving I quickly grabbed the pen and small pad and wrote down all the letters and the three numbers. EPHESIANS427 was what I had on the paper.

Mark grabbed it "EPHESIANS 427? What the hell is an Ephesians 427?"

"Sounds like a bible verse or something" Mark laughed.

It sounded familiar but I couldn't remember if I read anything in The Holy Bible with that title.

"Put your hands back on," Mark said.

"Dude, you're supposed to ask it a crazy question like, dear Ouija board, who is the next person that's going to die!" Before I could reply to Mark, our hands started to move again. Mark sat back and waited to see what I was going to write. I peeked over so I could see what I was going to have to write down. First letter it hovered over was M, and then it slowly moved to A. It was moving towards the next letter...

"Christian, Mark, I am ready now" Madam Vodsky called our names before I got to see the next letters.

"So what did it say?" Mark asked.

James Green

"I don't know, and Madam Vodsky called us before I could see the rest of it," I replied.

He nudged me on the shoulder on the way to the main table. "Hope it wasn't going to say me" he said with a smile.

Madam Vodsky looked at us with a small smile on her face, slowly blinking. "Now which one of you would like to go first?"

Mark quickly pointed at me. I laughed but in reality, I wanted to go first anyway.

"I would like to speak to my mother," I told her.

She nodded, "Very well." She closed her eyes; there was a silence in the room for five minutes maybe. It almost looked as she fell asleep. When I reached over to tap her, there was a gust of wind that came through the room. You could see the candles blowing, but none of them blew out. I could hear whispers all around me but I couldn't see where they were coming from. I saw a small crack of light forming on the wall in front of me. The crack got bigger and bigger until it looked like something was trying to come through.

"Christian"...I heard a voice coming from the wall. I looked over at Madam Vodsky but her head was still down as if she were sleep. I looked over at Mark and he was shivering with his eyes closed. The voice called me again as the light slowly came through the wall.

James Green

When the light came all the way through, it was too bright to look at. As the rays died down, I looked back and it was a woman. She was just hovering in the air like a ghost you would see on TV. As I focused in on her face, I couldn't believe it. It was my mother! She had a sad look on her face and the same running mascara as I pictured her.

"I love you my son," she said.

Her lips didn't move but her voice was clear. All the questions I had and I couldn't think of one because I was in shock. I didn't know what I was going to say but my lips opened. As soon as they opened she spoke again, "The girl...you must," but she was fading back towards the wall.

"MOM WAIT!" I called her as she was fading away, "WHAT GIRL?"

She was totally gone before I could hear her voice again. I could feel the tears forming in my eyes. That was the first time I had seen my mother since I was a child and I only got to see her for a few seconds. Madam Vodsky didn't wake up right away. My head was down towards the table but I could see the blond haired woman walking out. She stopped at the top of the stairs; I could feel her looking at me. When I looked up, she was gone.

Mark still had his eyes closed, "Is it over?" he asked.

James Green

"I saw my mom," I said with tears still in my eyes.

Madam Vodsky woke up, without acknowledging us, "Next, Tom Jennings please."

I stood and tapped Mark, "Let's go."

As we were walking up the stairs, Madam Vodsky spoke, "I will see you boys soon."

I paused but I didn't look back at her. I left her house with the total opposite feeling of what I expected to feel. I wanted to leave with clarity, with conclusion. Now I was just more confused and now I wanted to know more.

I started wondering was there anything left in my old burned down house. Was there a new house built or were there still remains of the old house? I realized I didn't even know where the house was. I didn't know if it was close or far; or if I needed to walk or catch a cab. I decided to make that a project.

James Green

THE CONCERT

Today was the day of the concert. I had never been to one so I was pretty excited. I wanted Amy to be there but Mark could only score us two tickets. I was in my room getting dressed and ready to go when I heard my phone. It was a text from Amy. "Hey Christian, just wanted to tell you to have fun and be safe at the concert and please text me when you get back, I really have something I want to talk to you about." I was kind of curious now, what has she been trying to tell me anyway. I text her back "What is it you wanted to tell me?" She took a few minutes to text back so I finished putting my clothes on. Her text finally came in "I don't want to text it to you, I will just talk to you about it when I see you." I was a little confused and curious at the same time but I didn't think a big deal of it. I finished getting dressed and waited for Mark. Since he was taking so long, I figured I would read a little while I waited. I looked on the nightstand and my two books were sitting right next to each other. This situation was getting more and more weird now. I didn't understand how my books kept moving out of my stand. The Holy Bible sat to the left, the lamp was in the middle and Satan's Bibel sat on the right. The light seemed to be shining on the Holy Bible more for some reason. I picked up The Holy Bible and put it in my nightstand with the intentions to finish reading it one day, as soon as I finished and understood the other one. I began

James Green

to open the book but I felt something reach over me. It opened the book for me and turned the pages. When I looked at the page, it was a section called "Invitation." It talked about how you could only join a sect through invitation only. All I could think of was someone coming to my door in a black robe, with bloody invitation in his hand. I shook off the daydream and read some more. My door opened and Mark was standing there.

"Dude are you r..." the door quickly slammed in Mark's face. I ran to the door and opened it. Mark was standing there holding his nose. It was bleeding from the door hitting it.

"What the hell man, what did you do to that door?"

I didn't say anything I quickly took him to the bathroom to get cleaned up. I asked him if he wanted to go to a hospital. His nose was red but we were able to get blood to stop flowing.

"Dude I wouldn't miss this concert if that door took my fucking nose off, this is 'Death' we are talking about here."

I laughed then nudged him on the shoulder. "Ok tough guy lets go."

We finally made it to the arena where the concert was being held. We caught a cab since it was too far to walk. Everyone there looked crazy. People had paint all over their faces; they were wearing

James Green

black wings. Some people were carrying around pitchforks and making noises I can't even describe. Everyone seemed to smell of alcohol and sweat. Lucky for us, our tickets were close to the front right in the middle of the floor...the exact same spot all the crazy people had their tickets.

When the show finally started, all the lights went out before the band came out. The leader of the band Jethro Baine appeared in the middle of the stage with the spotlight on him. Everyone was cheering. I was clapping but for some reason I was trying to focus in on him. He seemed to be praying, I could see his lips moving but I couldn't tell what he was saying. When he looked up, he gave a loud scream! There were fireworks and the band appeared behind him. Behind the band, there was a big black pyramid on the screen. It had an eye on the top of it; it looked the same as the one I seen on a dollar bill. The band started playing and the place went wild. I didn't know the words to any of the songs but I was dancing along with Mark playing air guitar and all the other stupid things people do at rock concerts. During the sixth song, Jethro was running all across the stage. He stopped in the middle and looked out at the crowd. It seemed like he was looking directly at me. He then appeared to point directly at me, as he was finishing the verse...all I heard was "yooooou willll seeeee." I imagine I was the only one that thought that was strange. I looked up to the top of the mega screen and I couldn't believe what I saw. It was the presence. He was just sitting there, seemingly enjoying the show.

James Green

When it seemed like his head was turning towards me his wings spread. I opened my mouth to say who knows what, when Mark bumped me. He was so into the concert and still dancing he didn't notice anything. I decided to just play along, get back into the concert and try to ignore what I saw. I was just hoping no one got hurt.

When the show was over, we were exhausted. All the air guitar and jumping around took a lot out of me. We stood in front of the arena waiting for a cab to come. A large black van pulled in front of us. I had never seen this kind of van before in my life. All I knew is that it looked expensive. The back window actually rolled down, I didn't know they made vans like that.

"Hey, you two, come here!" a guy with an English accent called out to us. We ran up to the van and it was Jethro Baine! What did he want with us? He asked us what we were doing for the rest of the night. We tried to sound important naming random things we planned on doing; we actually had nothing to do. "Why don't you two come grab a bite to eat with me...my treat?" he said.

We asked him should we catch a cab and meet him wherever he wanted to eat.

"No of course not, hop in," he told us. We sat in the back of the van expecting to see the whole band. It was just Jethro.

James Green

"Hey boys," a female voice came from the front seat of the van. I turned around to see who it was and it was the blonde haired woman we saw from Madam Vodsky's house.

"Fellas, this is my lovely wife Diana," Jethro said with a huge grin on his face. The rest of the ride we didn't say too much. Jethro was on the phone and Mark and I just listened to music; Death was playing on the CD player of course.

We pulled up to this huge, amazing restaurant. It looked like a castle with spotlights all around it, and expensive cars pulling up to the front door. I could see everyone was dressed in suits or tuxedos. Mark and I had on our clothes we wore at the concert, some jeans and a tee shirt. "Aren't we a little underdressed to get in?" I asked Jethro. "No worries men, you're with me," he said as we got out of the van. As soon as we exited the van, there were cameras flashing and people talking and asking questions. It was too many voices for me to understand any of them. It instantly made me realize I would never want to be famous, rich maybe, but not famous. We got to the door finally and we were greeted by a guy in a black tuxedo. He had a white cloth hanging over his forearm.

"Good evening Mr. Jethro, your table awaits you." We got a table that looked like it was for ten people but it was only four of us. Mark and I sat on one side, Jethro and his wife sat directly across from us. His wife Diana was so beautiful; she gave me the same butterflies as

James Green

Amy did when I looked at her. I suddenly remembered what happened last time I got caught staring too long and looked at my menu.

"So, boys" Jethro spoke. He didn't even look at the menu; the waiter already knew what to bring him. "My wife tells me you guys are regulars at the spiritual council meetings," he laughs a little and leans forward, "you guys don't believe in that stuff do you, like you think you're really talking to your dead mother?"

I had a confused look on my face, "I don't understand." Jethro looks at his wife and smiles.

"Never mind that, my wife likes to go here and there, it gives her comfort, she thinks it helps people, gives them a sense of peace. So tell me, do you like stuff like this?" He looked up at the ceiling then he looked towards the door where there was a guy coming in being escorted by two women. "The money, the toys, the women all that stuff?" he asked.

Mark and I looked at each other as if he had asked us the dumbest question in the world, "YES" we said simultaneously.

Jethro nodded and said, "Let me ask you guys, how do you guys think I got all of this, the money, the fame?"

I replied, "With good luck and hard work. "

James Green

Mark said by being a good singer.

Jethro laughed so hard at our responses he started holding his stomach. "A good singer he says; it's Mark right?" he said looking at Mark. "I can't sing worth shit. No one...and I mean no one gets anywhere in this world, without a higher power working for them."

There was a short silence, "You mean like, God?" I asked.

Jethro laughed again "Like God (he mocked me), I've been sent here to meet you guys and invite you to a meeting. I'd gladly take you but I'll be on tour so you'll have to find a way there," he wrote down an address on a napkin and slid it to us.

"How did you know how to find us?" I asked.

He told us that he was led there and that he knew where we were going to be, even where we were going to be standing at the concert. It made me think maybe he was really looking at me and pointing at me during that song. Mark seemed to be really impressed with all the money and women and things like that. He had this big smile on his face, as if we had got our big break in Hollywood or something. Our food came; it was brought out by four different waiters. There were steaks, shrimp, bread I had never seen before, a big salad, sushi, crab legs, lobster, everything else I'd never seen before so I couldn't tell you what it was. We ate and for the rest of the time it was only small talk. The bill came, the waiter slid it past me and I saw the

James Green

total, two thousand dollars! My eyebrows rose like I saw something wrong.

Jethro pulled out a big wad of cash and threw it on the table, "Alright lets go boys." We met the van at the front door. We hopped in and he took us home. We said thank you as we got out, he called out to us before he pulled off, "Don't forget the meeting boys." He waved and threw us a big wad of cash as the van pulled off. It must have been five thousand dollars! We were high school kids so that kind of money made us feel like millionaires. First thing I thought was that I was quitting my job, immediately! Next, I could buy Amy something nice, maybe something she could show off at prom and that I could get even a nicer suit for prom than my previous budget allowed. As we walked back to our rooms I wondered if we went to those meetings, would we be getting cash like this regularly? I always wanted a red Ferrari and with this kind of money, I could get one for sure! I would be the coolest kid in high school.

James Green

THE LOVE OF MONEY

The next day I quit my job. I didn't call to quit I just assumed they wouldn'tice that I never came back. I remembered my measurements from the store so I ordered a suit for prom from this website where they sold expensive suits. I ordered a pair of expensive shoes and a belt too. I sat there trying to think of things I could buy that I couldn't afford before. Before I got carried away, I remembered I wanted to get Amy something. I had no idea what to get her so I figured I would try to probe her for information and see what she liked.

The next day at school, I had a different walk. I actually had of a smile on my face. Having money in my pocket gave me a different feeling. I was confident, I felt cooler. I had every single dollar I had left in my pocket so you could see a little bulge on my thigh. I ran into Amy in the hallway, "Hey baby," I said as I leaned on the locker next to hers. She looked at me with a strange look. "What's got into you?" I told her that I missed her and asked her what she wanted to talk to me about. She paused for a second and told me that it wasn't a good time to talk about it. I started to feel a little concerned and even more curious. I changed the subject anyway and told her I ordered my suit for prom. What I didn't tell her is I reserved us a Rolls Royce, which cost me $300 an hour. I wanted to keep that a surprise though.

James Green

"So, what would be the perfect gift for the perfect girl?" I asked her. I'm not that great of an actor so I could tell she already knew I wanted to buy her something.

"I don't want anything, as long as I have you," she said as she touched my cheek.

"Oh yeah! Guess what! You'll never believe what happened to me and Mark!" I told her how we met Jethro after the Death concert and about the dinner he took us to. I left out the part about the money and the meeting we were invited to. I know I should have been sharing everything with her but I was too scared. I didn't know what she would think of me. I was going to tell her one day though, just didn't know exactly when. It was a good thing she didn't want a gift, it seemed my money wasn't as abundant as when I first got it. I had already quit my job, now I just had to find another way to get some more. All I could think of is if I went to that meeting, then that would be the way.

When I got home, I went to check with Mark to see if he was going to the meeting with me. It didn't matter if he was going or not, I was going anyway; plus I needed some more money. Fortunately, he was as excited as I was and had about as much money left as I did. I could see in his room he had a new flat screen, a new game system, some new clothes, I even saw a gold watch.

"Been spending I see," I laughed.

James Green

Mark laughed too "Well, maybe a little."

The meeting was set for that weekend. I looked on the internet and saw we would have to catch a cab to get there, it was entirely too far to walk. I had no idea what it was going to be like. Was it going to be a bunch of rock stars? Then it hit me...I thought about what kind of meeting this was. I remembered about what I read as far as being rewarded for doing things I wouldn't imagine doing. I thought about the money and decided to take a chance anyway. Maybe it wouldn't be that bad; maybe we would go to the meeting and they will give us some money just for coming.

James Green

THE MEETING

It was Sunday, the day of the meeting. Mark and I were up early because we were so anxious. All we could think and talk about was what we were going to do with our next five thousand dollars. I even told him eventually I wanted to get a red Ferrari. It's amazing what a high school kid can think of to do with money. I'm sure they were all dumb ideas, but they sounded genius to us.

The cab picked us up, and we were on our way. We were about an hour away and everything started to look different. The houses were getting bigger, the cars were more expensive, and the streets were cleaner. It took about an hour and a half before we pulled up to our destination. I wish I could describe how big this house actually was. If I said it looked like two houses combined, I wouldn't be doing it any justice. Mark and I split the cab fare since it was so high. I tried to block the thought of having to pay that again to get home.

We walked towards the front door. There were huge fountains with angels spitting water. The grass was so green and beautiful. The bushes were cut to perfection. You could smell the flowers that were planted around the area. There were at least 20 cars lined up in front of the house and they all fit perfectly. It wasn't too crowded or anything. Every car was a Porsche, a Lamborghini, a Rolls

James Green

Royce, a Mercedes or an Audi; then I saw my baby. Someone had a red
Ferrari 599 GTB, just like the one I'd been thinking about every day.
"Come on let's go!" I was so excited I rushed Mark to get to the front
door. I rang the doorbell. The butler opened the door, he had a big
mustache.

"Hello, May I help you," he said. I expected him to know who
we were like Madam Vodsky did but I was mistaken.

"Um, we were invited my Jethro, you know from the rock band
Death, he told us to come here today," I said nervously. He looked us
up and down, and then he pulled a list out of his pocket. "Mark and
Christian," I said as he was looking at the list. As we stood there, he
didn't look up and acknowledge us at all.

"Maybe we have the wrong place?" I tapped Mark and began
to walk away.

"Wait!" the butler said. When we turned around, he had a
smile on his face. "I was only kidding my boys, come on in." When we
walked in, the house looked like museum. There were pictures and
statues everywhere. All the pictures were of Angels. They were a
little different then what I saw on the internet, these were much more
beautiful. The pictures looked real, as if someone was painting a model
posed as an angel. We got to the kitchen and there were people
standing there talking and snacking. I realized why the butler looked

James Green

us up and down then. Everyone had on suits like they were on their way to that restaurant Jethro took us to. I had on a black tee shirt, a black pair of jeans and some black shoes. No one seemed to care though; everyone shook our hands and smiled. Everyone was polite and welcoming. One man approached us; he had on a nice black suit and a nice pair of glasses. He introduced himself, he told us he was a doctor and that he would introduce us to some of the people there. Everyone there seemed to be a doctor, a lawyer, a surgeon, a singer, or an actor. It was kind of intimidating but exciting at the same time.

There was a huge clock in the living room. I wanted a closer look because I had never seen a clock that huge. The time read 6:35. The hands looked like skinny wings. When it struck 6:36, an alarm sounded. Everyone started heading in one direction. Mark and I had no idea what to do so we just followed the crowd. We walked down a long hallway; both walls were made of glass. You could see outside but the sun rays didn't come in enough to make it too bright or too hot in there, it was amazing. As we were walking, I looked to my right at my reflection. I smiled at myself thinking how lucky I was to be there. I looked back to see Marks reflection, suddenly I got startled. I saw Mark walking with blood pouring down from his neck as if someone had cut it open. I was so startled I fell on the floor.

"What's wrong dude?" Mark reached down to help me up.

"Um, nothing, I just tripped."

James Green

Mark knew by now I was a bad liar. He shook his head "Come on dude, we're falling behind." We caught up with the group and we ended up in a room that was about as big as a basketball court. As I looked around, I noticed it reminded me of a church. It had nice benches and a podium up front for someone to speak. There were more statues and pictures all around. There was one picture in the center of the main wall. It was the largest picture in the house. The angel was so beautiful. You could see the wisdom and power in his face. It was amazing. It seemed like it was staring right at me. We all took a seat. Mark and I sat in the back trying not to draw too much attention to ourselves. Once everyone took a seat, a man stepped up to the podium, and then he began to speak.

James Green

THE SERMON (part 1)

Hello everyone, most of you know who I am already; but for our special guests today, I would like to introduce myself. My name is Doctor Halsted. Before we get started with today's service, we usually take a little time to give testimony. Some of us share what the spirits' have done for us recently. If I am not mistaken it is my turn to give the first testimony.

Well this past Wednesday I had to perform a major, major heart surgery. The patient had been on the donor list for some time. My team and I were in the operation room. Before we started we all held hands as I spoke to the spirits, asking them to guide my hands in this surgery. When we let go, I felt the spirits take a hold of my hands. They were moving my arms as if I were a puppet. I opened the patient's chest; I could see her heart was at least double in size. As I began to cut out the old heart, I noticed all blood had stopped flowing. There was no blood to clean out the way or anything. It made it much easier and faster to remove the old heart. Putting in the new heart was surprisingly easy too. When everything was stitched back together, the blood started flowing again as if it never stopped. The patient became stable and she was good as new. The word spread about the young woman's surgery and now I have hundreds of patients in line now waiting for me to help them. *Everyone claps.* Thank you, now by

James Green

the show of hands how many of you make at least six figures? *Everyone raised their hand and Doctor Halsted smiles.* Now, by the show of hands, how many of you make at least seven figures? *Half of the audience raised their hand.* Good, good, now is there anyone that would like to give their testimony for the week? *A woman raised her hand; she wore big sunglasses and a scarf around her head. She had the look of a movie star. She stands up and walks to the front. She tapped the microphone to make sure the sound was right, and then she spoke.*

"Hello everyone, for those of you who don't know me my name is Lauren Lyn. I am a country western singer. I have been in the business about five years now. In the beginning, my career wasn't going so well. People didn't like my voice and I couldn't get many venues to book any of my shows. When I first started, I used to open up for my best friend. She was a much better singer than I was. Back then, we were both 18, but she could pack a place like no one's business. In her spare time, she would always help me with my music. We would work on things like getting my voice better and we would also work on my guitar playing. One day we were headed to a show in Dallas. We decided to drive instead of fly to save a little money and have some girl time together. We had about a half tank of gas left but she wanted to get off the freeway and fill up anyway. I told her we should keep going, but she insisted because she said she was hungry. I was sitting in

James Green

the passenger seat while she began to pump the gas. The nozzle seemed to be jammed a little so she had to give it a tug to get it out.

"When it finally gave way, gas spewed out all over her clothes. She was always one of those people that never got mad so she laughed it off and began pumping the gas. We were laughing and joking while the tank was filling up when I could see a guy come out of the gas station. He had a strange look to him. He had a sandwich in one hand and a lighter in the other. Usually that would be no big deal but he also had a cigarette hanging from his lip. It all seemed like it was going in slow motion. I was still talking to my friend but my eyes were on the man. His eyes were directly on me as he lit the cigarette. His eyes then turned to my friend, before I could call her name he flicked the cigarette at her and she caught a flame. Her scream was so agonizing it put me into shock. I didn't know what to do but sit there and scream. By the time the fire truck and ambulance got there, it was much too late. She was so burned I couldn't bear to look at her. Before they took her car, something told me to look in the armrest. There was a piece of paper that had the address to this place, this church. I put it in my pocket and let them take the car. I ended up missing the show because I was so devastated by what happened. They never caught the man that threw the cigarette either. I started coming here in hopes I could follow my best friends path. I made it my goal to be just like her or even better.

James Green

"I was finally lucky enough to get booked for a show; it was as if it came out of nowhere. I was so excited, but then I realized, my voice was gone. I had lost my voice the day before. I couldn't cancel the show though, it was my only shot. I remember what I learned and asked the spirits for help. When it was time to step on stage I sat in my chair and held my guitar in my hand. I was nervous. Before I opened my mouth, I could see something coming towards me. As it got closer, I could see it was my best friend. She had a huge smile. My mouth opened a little and she flew right in. It looked as if I got hit in the chest by a 300-pound man. All of a sudden, I felt her take over. I reached for the microphone and my voice came out more beautiful than it ever had my entire life. The crowd went crazy! After that show, I met a record company executive. He offered me a record deal on the spot. Here I am ten million dollars later. All thanks to the spirits." *Everyone claps.*

James Green

THE REACTION

After I heard Lauren Lyn's testimony, I was convinced. I pictured myself in my red Ferrari, I pictured me buying Amy a huge wedding ring, and I pictured us pulling up to our huge mansion. I looked over at Mark but he didn't look as excited as I did. He looked as everything sounded good, but there had to be something wrong. I could tell by the way he was trying to smile. I was so excited I didn't pay attention to the rest of the sermon.

After the service, Doctor Halsted approached us. "So, what did you guys think?"

I told him it was nice and I was excited and intrigued by the testimonies I heard. I decided to ask a direct and bold question. "So, you all, you all worship the Devil?"

Dr. Halsted laughs and puts his hand on my shoulder, "Lucifer, yes, our master, he is our lord."

I asked why with a confused look on my face, "Isn't he evil?"

He smiled at me but looked prepared to answer the question. "Evil, no my friend, not at all. The story you've heard about what happened in Heaven, it was all a big misunderstanding. This isn't a

James Green

battle of good and evil, this is simply a small fight between two sides. One side has their version of the story and the other has theirs. In the end, Jesus will take his people and advocate the world to Lucifer since it is rightfully his anyway. It is against God's nature to destroy Lucifer so the story you've heard is false. "

I was really confused at this time but I wanted to ask one more question before I left, "What about hell, isn't God going to send you all to hell?"

He looked at me and nodded a little, "There are no worries about hell, and the spirits can outlive fire. Haven't you seen people walk on fire? Where do you think they get that ability from? You come back next week, and think of anything you want to the spirits to do for you. When you come back, tell me what you want and it will be given to you. "

He handed me a piece of paper; it was an appointment slip to come back the next Sunday. I was surprised how quiet Mark was. As we walked out the door Dr. Halsted called to us, "Hey boys! Just in case you need something to get back with," he threw us a wad of cash. I flipped my fingers through it and it was twenty-five hundred dollars. I could see that the site of cash made Mark feel a little better about everything. The ride home was quiet at first. I was counting the money thinking about what to buy and Mark just stared out the window.

James Green

"What's wrong dude?" I wanted to know what was on Mark's mind.

"I don't know man, the Devil, hell? Is money worth going to hell? Don't get me wrong I like the money and I like nice things...but at what cost you know?"

I could tell by the tone of his voice he was serious. The feeling was a lot different for me with the money just sitting in my hand. I looked down for a second, and then I had suddenly came up with a clever idea.

"How about we just keep the money, but don't get into all that worship and things like that." The way I said it you might have thought it was a genius idea, but Mark didn't smile, he just looked back out the window, "I don't know man."

James Green

THE FIRST TIME

The next day I went out to buy Amy a necklace. I thought if I bought her a ring, it would be too much. I found a nice diamond necklace with a heart pendant that I thought would look perfect on her. I invited her over that night to give it to her. When she came in, she looked a little nervous.

"You ok?" I asked.

She told me she was fine and that she still wanted to tell me something and it was important.

I smiled and said, "Wait, me first." I pulled out the small box with the necklace from behind my back and handed it to her.

"What's this?" she asked.

"Just open it," I said, I was smiling ear to ear. When she opened it, her eyes lit up like two beautiful stars. I could see tears forming in her eyes, "This is beautiful Christian, thank you...where did you get the money for this?" she asked. I told her I had just saved up; I never told her I quit my job. She reached out and hugged me real tight. We started to kiss as she kicked my door closed. She threw the

James Green

box on my chair. She stared at me while she began to take her coat off. Before I could take a step forward, she took her shirt off.

I never had sex before so I didn't know if this was about to happen or if this was the cue to take my clothes off or just watch. She stepped forward and took my shirt off. As she took her jeans off I assumed I should take mine off. We kissed again and fell on the bed. I looked over at my other pillow and I saw a book laying there. I grabbed it, and saw it was The Holy Bible before I put it on my nightstand. When I looked back at Amy, I saw the presence standing at the foot of the bed. I began to shiver with fear but I didn't want Amy to know so I kissed her. I knew by now that it was the presence of the Devil. It only made sense now. As we kissed I heard a deep voice:

"YOU WERE WARNED."

I quickly opened my eyes and saw the Devil walking slowly towards the window. As he flew out the window, I assumed Amy saw and heard everything.

"What is it?" she asked.

To my surprise, she didn't hear anything. We kissed again and for the first time, we made love. I know as high school kids we were too young, but the whole moment felt right, it was perfect.

James Green

She had to leave later on that night. When we kissed goodbye, Mark came out of his room with a funny grin. I imagine he could tell what just happened.

He punched me in the shoulder, "Nice" he said. "Anyway, I thought about it and I want to go to the next meeting, or church, or whatever it is they do there. I just want to make enough money and get out. There is no telling what happens if we stay there forever."

I told him I agreed and we decided to go to the next service.

James Green

THE SERMON (part 2)

Sunday came around again, which meant it was time for the next service. I was up early that day. I think I was just anxious and hoping we were going to get some more money just for coming again. I was dressed before Mark so I decided to catch up on some reading. I reached behind me where I knew my Satanic Bibel was. When I brought it forward, I noticed it was The Holy Bible. It made me wonder, why this book was popping up everywhere? I knew I wasn't moving it and I know no one was in my room moving the book for no reason.

I took my thumb and just opened the book to whatever page it was going to take me too. I looked in the top right corner of the book and saw that it was the book of Ephesians chapter four. I quickly turned to chapter twenty-seven, "neither give place to the devil," it said. I remembered the Ouija board; I remembered the girl in the hallway. Everything in the world told me to listen and read more but I couldn't. The thought of more money and Amy blinded me. I put the book away once again as Mark opened my door, "I'm ready," he said as I got up and grabbed my jacket.

Fortunately, we still had enough money to get there and back. It was the same long ride, this time though, we were both quiet. I knew

James Green

what I wanted, but I started to wonder that if I got everything I wanted, at what cost was it going to come with. I still had the Ouija board in the back of my mind; I knew it was spelling Mark after he asked it who was going to die next.

We arrived and walked to the front door. The butler didn't joke around with us as he did the last time, probably because of the look on our faces. We stood around drinking their juice, eating the little snacks they had available and speaking to whomever spoke to us. Everyone was as polite as they were the first time we went. I saw Dr. Halsted wave to us from across the room, he had a few men gathered around him. It looked like they were talking about something important so I didn't walk over. The clock struck six and everyone headed toward the room where they held their service. Mark and I sat in the back again hoping no one would call on us to say anything.

Dr. Halsted started off the same way he did the last time. He opened by saying that it was time to give testimony about what the spirits had done for them recently. He asked would anyone like to go first. A man raised his hand. He had black hair and a really nice grey suit on. He got to the podium looked out to the crowd, and then he spoke...

"Good evening everyone, my name is Peter Fenway. I just wanted to take a little time to tell you all what the spirits have done for me this past week. I own a few coffee shops that earn me a good

James Green

amount of money. Business has always been good since I've been coming here. As time went by, I had what you might want to call a gambling problem. Even though I make over a hundred grand a year, I blow most of it at the casino. About two weeks ago, I decided to ask the spirits for more help. They had already been helping me with my coffee shops but I wanted even more help. I wanted to win at the casino. I wanted to get that high of winning and winning big. I asked them to help me win at blackjack. Last Wednesday I took about ten grand with me and took a ride to the casino. Before I went in, I talked to the spirits reminding them what I had asked for (*he laughs*). When I got to the table, I put down one hundred dollars on my first bet. The dealer deals me a fifteen and he has a seven. Basic strategy tells me to take a hit so I do so...I bust.

Now I'm really angry because I thought the spirits ignored me, but something told me to put down more money the next time. I put down two grand on the next hand and I won ten straight blackjacks. At the end of the night, I walked out of there with one hundred grand! I made a year's worth of money in that one night. I am proof at what the spirits can do for you!" (*Everyone claps*)

Whatever doubts Mark and I had were clearly forgotten about at that moment. We looked at each other, "One hundred grand" we said at the same time. I knew I was going to pay attention to the rest of the service this time. I kept getting a small uncomfortable feeling

James Green

because it felt like that big picture in the middle was looking at me. Someone was a good artist because the painting looked almost too real.

Dr. Halsted walked back to the podium and began the sermon; it was a sermon I would never forget. He stood at the podium looked out to the crowd, and then he spoke...

"Today we are going to discuss a few important points. The master has guided me into the discussion for today because he wanted everyone to be clear of our plan. If we don't follow it to the letter, we will fail. Does anyone know about the Great Council that was held back in the 1700's? (*No one raised their hand*) The master is a wise individual. He has studied The Holy Bible more than any human being on Earth has. The Great Council held in the 1700's regarded a plan. The master and his angels devised a way whereby people would basically disqualify themselves from being members of Christ's kingdom. There were three policies discussed, and I shall go over them with you. Policy number one: Deceive the people about the angels and Lucifer's existence. If you don't believe in the existence of Lucifer, why would you have any reason to believe in the Creator?

"If you can discredit one thing in The Holy Bible, you can discredit the entire book. Now, have we been successful in that area? Survey says Seventy five percent , are you all listening? Seventy five percent of people don't believe in a tangible Devil; that is astounding. Policy number two: Take control over the minds of people through

James Green

hypnotism. The plan was to take it out of the realm of the occult and introduce it as a science for the benefit of mankind. The term mesmerism was brought about. It basically stated that people had some kind of magnetism, which allowed them to put a "trans" on others. It was and is widely accepted by the public. (*He laughs*) People really do believe anything don't they? People actually believe the Earth is billions and billions and billions of years old. If you do the math from the time of creation, the Earth is only six thousand years old. (*The crowd is silent*) Can you believe that? (*Brief pause*) Policy number three: Policy number three says we must destroy The Holy Bible...without burning it. Now how does that happen? The master chose Charles Darwin. He personally taught him how to set up the principles of the Theory of Evolution. If a person believes in Evolution, it destroys the creation week in The Holy Bible, the fall of man, and the plan of redemption! Anyone who teaches the Theory of Evolution is considered to be a minister of our great religious system. He is of great value, he will receive unction from Lucifer himself and will receive great power with the ability to convert, convince, and to induce spiritual blindness. He will also be assigned angels to follow him the rest of his life, which is considered the greatest gift from the master. (*He smiles*)

"I also wanted to go over, who all here is familiar with Lucis Trust located in the United Nations." (*Half the audience raised their hand*) Well Lucis Trust was known before as Lucifer Trust. It was

founded by Alice A. Bailey. She is considered one of our great leaders in our religion. In one of her twenty-five esoteric books, she came up with The Ten Strategies to Get Occult Principles to be accepted by the world. This was a plan carefully thought out and guided by the master. In my opinion, it is genius. Number 1: Push God out of schools, if people grow up without a reference to God, they will consider God irrelevant. Number 2: Break traditional Christian family concepts. Break communication between parents and children so that parents can't pass on spiritual values to their children. You accomplish this by pushing excessive child rights. Number 3: Remove restrictions on sex. Sex is the biggest joy and Christianity robs people of this. People must be free to enjoy it without restrictions. It is not just for the married, it is for everybody.

"Number 4: Sex is the greatest expression of a man's enjoyment of life. Man must be free to express sex in all its forms; homosexuality, orgies, even beastiality are desirable as long as no one is harmed or abused. Number 5: People must be free to abort unwanted children. Number 6: Every person develops soul bonds. Therefore, when a soul bond wears out, a person must be free to divorce. When one starts to grow one must be free to get together with that person even if they are married. Number 7: Defuse religion radicalism. Christianity says Jesus is the only way; defuse this by: a) silencing Christianity; and b) promoting other faiths, the creation of interfaith harmony. Number 8: Use the media to influence mass opinion. Create mass opinion that is

receptive to these values by using TV, Film, the press and so forth.
Note, what western believers call normal, in the African church would
be considered pornography. Number 9: Debase art in all its forms.
Corrupt music, paintings, poetry to every expression of the heart and
make it obscene, immoral, and occultic. Debase the arts in every way
possible. (*Long pause*) And Number 10: Get the church to endorse all
nine strategies. Get the church to accept these principles and say that
they are ok. Then legal ground is given for these values to get a
foothold.

"Good stuff huh? Our plan is being followed to the T! There is
no doubt in my mind that we will be victorious. I don't want to keep
you all day but I want to go over one more topic.

"The Grand plan before the end of the Great Controversy.
(*He smiles*) People are going to just eat this up. Angels will declare
themselves to be inhabitants of far distant planets. A threat will be
made that people will be destroyed if they don't follow the instructions
given to them. The angels will give guidance in avoiding the
destruction of the planet and cause it to enter a higher state of
existence. A glorious new age of peace and prosperity will come to last
one thousand years if instructions are carried out correctly. There will
be no wars, no famine, no social unrest, just love. As the times get
harder and harder the angels will impress the importance of Sunday
sacredness. Laws will be passed to honor Sunday. The police will

James Green

explain to the masses that the law is necessary to assure the well being of all people.

"Now I know that was a lot for one day, but are there any questions? (*One man raises his hand*)

"Is it true that the spirits helped the founder of Coca Cola?"

"Yes, it is one hundred percent true. You see Coca Cola had a deal with the master. The master told him "I will make you the number one business, the most powerful on Earth; but every month you must offer me three souls in sacrifice." Those souls ended up being sacrificed and bottled. This came out with a guy in Germany many years ago; he found fingers and the remains of flesh inside bottles of coke. It was a price the founder was willing to pay to be powerful and wealthy."

(*Another man raised his hand*)

"What about the Adventists?"

"What about them?"

"How do they play a role in our plan when they observe the Sabbath?"

Dr. Halsted laughs, "oh yeah, the Adventists. Most Adventists cannot be brought under our great deception. However, it really doesn't matter since there are only a few of them. That fact that

James Green

they observe the day of the creator makes it impossible for the spirits to deceive them. They are not ordinary people, they have spiritual insight. But they are nothing to worry about. Now, are there any more questions? (*No one raised their hand*)Good, good, I think we covered a lot today. I think we all know now that we have a lot of work to do, for the time is short at hand...thank you. " (*He steps down*)

James Green

THE CONSEQUENCE

When the sermon was over there was a mixture of feelings inside it almost made me sick. I had an overwhelming feeling of wanting money; but at the same time hearing the plans of those people were disturbing, and almost not worth the thought of taking any money or asking any spirits to do anything. I knew I was probably going to continue coming. All signs in the world said I should leave this place and never look back, but I had a good idea that it wouldn't be that easy, especially after hearing all the information we heard. I looked over at Mark and he was just staring at the huge picture on the main wall. He had fear and tears in his eyes. He looked over at me and shook his head, "I can't do it bro, this can't be right."

I didn't respond with any words, all I did was shake my head as if I agreed with him.

We got up to leave and as we headed for the front door Dr. Halsted stopped us. "Hey boys, I know that was a lot to digest today, might even have been a little overwhelming. But the master tells me you boys are more than ready to join our army and help us fight for our cause. I am inclined to tell you that after today, how can I put this...there is no way out. You are a part of our family now. No worries boys, the spirits will make it worth your while." As he was finishing up

James Green

his motivational speech, I could feel him slipping something in my pocket. I knew it was money. He knew the kind of money he was giving us would blind us, well me anyway.

Dr. Halsted sent us home in a limo this time instead of letting us catch a cab. We didn't have to pay for it so I didn't have to take any money out of the stash I had in my pocket. On the way home, I could see the tears in Mark's eyes.

"You ok?" I asked him.

He took a second to respond, "Did you hear any of that that went on in there? Do you see what they are doing to us, doing to everyone? I like money and all Christian, but I can't go to hell over it. "

I didn't know what to say because I knew I was going back. "So there's no way you're going back there, not even to see what those spirits can do for you?" I asked.

"No way," he said in a definitive voice.

When he said that I got a chill up my back and there was a small gust of wind that came through the back of the limo. I looked around and saw no windows were down. I looked over at the window and noticed I couldn't see my reflection. I leaned a little bit forward and I could see the black figure that was blocking my reflection. *No* I said to myself. All I could think about was the Ouija board. I closed

James Green

my eyes; I just knew the devil was going to do something to Mark; I balled my fists and yelled…"NO!" I still had my eyes closed but I didn't hear anything. When I opened them, I noticed Mark was just staring at me as if I was crazy.

"Dude, you need some serious medication. I forgot I had to go to my grandmothers today, I wonder if the driver will drop me off there." He knocked on the glass that separated us from the driver and asked him could he drop him off at a different address. The driver gave him a thumbs up. Although I was a little embarrassed, I was greatly relieved that nothing happened to him. Even though he was my only friend, I considered him my best friend.

When we arrived to his grandparents' house, I noticed it was darker outside. It wasn't nighttime but the clouds moved over the sun and gave the illusion that it was. We shook hands and he got out. The limo driver was waiting until he made it in the house; I guess he wanted to make sure he didn't have to come back. By the time Mark reached the sidewalk, I forgot to give him half of the money I had in my pocket. I rolled down the window and called his name "Mark!" He turned around and saw the money I was holding in my hand. He started to head back towards the car. He walked to the middle of the street, "Just toss it to me I don't feel like walking back over." I laughed as I took his half and put it in the rubber band that it came in. I reached my arm out the window and tossed him the wad of money. Before his fingertips

James Green

could grab the money, an SUV suddenly hit Mark. It came by so fast that it looked like Mark exploded. All I could see was blood and money floating in the air. The truck didn't even turn around to see what happened. "Mark Noooooooooooooooo" I screamed as I jumped out of the car. I fell to my knees with my face buried in my hands. I don't know why I did, but I looked up to the sky. I could see the Devil standing on top of Mark's grandparents' house. I couldn't see his but I know we locked eyes. He had to have felt the instant hate I had for him. Mark was the only friend I ever had; and he took that away from me. Maybe it was the wrong feeling to have; but I knew I was going to make all the money I could off the spirits and then I was going to leave that God forsaken place.

I figured if he was going to hurt me, he would've already done it. I don't know why he was even following me in the first place but I didn't care anymore. My obsession with the Devil suddenly got stronger. The limo driver blew his horn for me to get back in. I ignored his heartlessness for the situation and got back in. I didn't want to be bothered with the police anyway.

When I got back home, I walked straight to my room. There was blood all over my pants but no one seemed to notice. No one even asked where Mark was. I got to my room, sat in my chair, and I started thinking. I knew there was something that had to be done, I just didn't know what.

James Green

THE PROM AND THE DREAM

It was finally time for prom, what all the seniors in high school were waiting for. All the tuxes and cars and the excitement was all about this one day. I admit, Amy was so excited about the whole thing that it made me excited. By now, I had enough money to do whatever I wanted. I had an expensive suit on, I rented a Rolls Royce for the weekend, and it felt like I had it all.

It had been two weeks since Mark was killed. He had been reported missing but strangely no detectives or anybody asked me anything. I felt untouchable. During those two weeks, I returned to hear Dr. Halsted speak twice. Within that time, I asked the spirits for money. I had only asked once, but when I asked, I asked for fifty thousand dollars. I didn't know what to do after I asked. I didn't know if I should go play the lottery or go to the casino. When I got home from service that day I went to my room to ponder on how to get the money. To my surprise when I looked on my bed there were one hundred dollar bills piled up next to my pillow. Under all the bills, there was a little note, "FOR YOU," it said. I threw the note away and didn't feel a bit of thanks. All I wanted to do was take. I left right back out and I went to pick up the Rolls Royce for prom.

Prom started at seven and it was about four thirty in the afternoon. I waited at home while Amy got dressed at her house. I was

James Green

always early doing things so I was already dressed. I decided to catch a little nap since it was going to be a long night. I reclined my chair, closed my eyes and fell asleep. Now I've had some crazy dreams before but the one I had then was an interesting one.

My eyes had opened, but they were only open in my dreams. I was sitting on a bench in the nearby woods. I stood to walk toward a undetermined destination, when I heard a voice, "Sit" it said. I looked behind me and it was an angel. He was dressed in white and he had a beautiful glow around him. Even though the wings looked familiar, I knew it wasn't the Devil right away. When I sat back down on the bench, he sat with me. He had a book in his hand. He opened it as if he wanted me to look inside. "Here is wisdom," he said. When I looked, I saw a Catholic priest. He was dressed in the usual white garments.

"I don't understand," I said to the angel.

"Keep looking" he responded. I looked back and I saw the priest changing his clothes. When he was changed he had on a black garment with the words "The Brotherhood" written on the back, and the whites of his eyes were gone; they were a deep dark black. He dipped his hand in some kind of tray and made a upside down cross on a woman's forehead. Suddenly words flashed, *Defeat, Rebellion, Christ*, and then I saw some kind of figure that looked like a man hanging from a cross. I had no idea what I was looking at but I wanted to see more. The angel turned the page. The next page was blank for a

James Green

second and words seemed to type themselves on the page...*Count The Number Of The Beast* it said. Then one at a time a six appeared on the page until it was three of them. Then two of them disappeared and the six turned into a dice. I saw the dice had six sides and had the numbers one through six. The dice then turned into dominoes. I saw that the dominoes went up to the number six. The angel turned the page again. This page was an empty chess board. The board took up both pages. On the top left corner of the left page was the word Christians, on the top right corner of the right page it said, Satanists.

"There is a war," said the angel. Suddenly six pieces one by one appeared on the side of the Satanists. A pawn appeared, the angel spoke, "They represent members of the satanic sects, they are sent out to all the congregations." The rook appeared, "They represent the Catholic Church, who protects the satanic sects." The bishop appeared, "The pope." The two knights appeared, "They will arise two demons, and they will fight against Christ during his second coming." The queen appeared, "The queen, she represents the Satanic Sects, you see how she is protected." Finally the king appeared, "The king, he is Lucifer, the Devil." I stared at the king and it started to change shape. It formed itself into the figure I've known all my life. I balled up my fist and went to hit the book. Before I could strike, my cell phone rang and I woke up startled.

James Green

It was Amy calling. I noticed it was six o'clock. I didn't realize I had slept for that long. She told me she had one stop to make and she was going to call me back so I could meet her at her house. It seemed kind of late, I knew people wanted to take pictures before we left.

"Oh, I have a surprise for you too," she said.

I laughed, "Oh yeah, are you going to tell me or are you going to keep it a secret like the other thing you were supposed to tell me a million years ago."

Her voice suddenly got more serious. "You're right, I'm sorry about that I just never found the right time to say, I promise I will tell you when you pick me up," she said.

I said ok and we hung up.

It was seven and Amy still hadn't called me back. I decided to drive over to her house anyway. I figured she might have still been getting ready since she was always so slow doing things. I noticed on the way to her house that the sky was darker. I was hoping it wasn't going to rain on our prom day. When I pulled up, I saw Amy's mom talking to the police. When he left, I could see her mother crying. I knew prom was a happy and emotional thing for women but she was crying a little too hard. I made it up to the steps where she was standing, "What's wrong ma'am?" I asked. She grabbed me and

James Green

hugged me real tight. It reminded me of the hug Amy gave me when Brad died.

"Christian," she said, she could barely get her words out, "Its Amy, she got in a car accident."

I quickly pushed away from her hug, "What?!" I said.

"She's at the hospital now, I'm waiting for her dad so we can ride up there together," she said.

I quickly ran to my car and headed to the hospital. I must have been doing ninety in a Rolls Royce.

I pulled up to the front of the hospital, I quickly ran out of the car, I left the car running I was in such a rush. When I got to the receptionist, I asked her where Amy was. "And you are?" she asked. I realized if I told her who I really was, she wasn't going to let me see her, "I'm her brother; I heard she just got in a car accident." She pointed down the hallway, "She's in 106," I ran down the hallway before she could hand me the sign in sheet. When I got there, I could see she was bloody and bruised. She had oxygen tubes stuck in her nose. I grabbed her hand softly hoping she would wake up. "Amy." I called her name, no response. "Amy please," I tried again, her eyes opened.

James Green

She smiled, "Christian, I'm sorry baby, I should've been paying more attention." She started to cry as I rubbed her hand and told her not to worry about anything and that everything was going to be ok.

"Christian, I have to tell you something, it's important."

Before I could respond I felt a gust of wind enter the room. I looked around expecting to see the devil somewhere but I didn't see anything. "Just get some rest Amy, you can tell me when you get better," I said as I kept rubbing her hand.

"NO, I have to tell you now! Please. Remember the house fire when you were younger?"

"Yes, why, what does that have to do with anything?"

"Well I looked up the article the night you told me and...the story doesn't match up Christian."

"What do you mean?"

"Christian, who was in the house that night?"

"Me, my mom...and my dad."

"Christian, it just said it was you and your mom. They didn't say anything about your dad."

"Amy, what are you talking about?"

James Green

"There is no record of your dad...anywhere."

I tried to remember everything I could about my father and came up with nothing. Who was this man, who was the man that walked out of my house that night? Amy began to cough and it looked like she was in pain. I kneeled down closer attempting to give her more comfort. I looked up and saw the Devil in the corner of the room. He stood in the exact same place he stood when I was a child in the hospital. I began to cry and turned back to Amy. I stroked her hair as she spoke again.

"Its one more thing I had to tell you Christian (*she coughs and the heart monitor starts to beep slower*)"

"Yes, what is it..."

"I'm...I'm pregnant. (*The heart monitor flat lines*)"

I let go of her hands turning around expecting to see the Devil; but he had already left the room. I stopped crying and saw there was some paper sticking out of Amy's purse. I opened it and it was the old article about the house fire. I quickly scanned the paper and saw the address. The house had to be about ten minutes walking distance from the hospital. I knew what I had to do then. I walked out the hospital as I saw Amy's parents rush past me to her room. They were in a panic; they didn't notice that they ran past me. I left the car out front and headed straight towards the house. I must have had a million emotions

James Green

running through me. I didn't know if there was going to be anything there, a new house built or a pile of ash.

When I got there, I could see the house was still standing. About ninety percent of the house was blackened where it had burned. I couldn't help wonder why did they leave the house standing after all these years. I stood at the front door and said three words I should've said a long time ago..."God help me." It's hard to describe what I felt after I said those words but I felt the feeling as if a large amount of pressure was lifted from my shoulders. I walked in the house unafraid, not knowing what I would find.

When I walked in, I saw right away the upstairs had fallen downstairs, just as I remembered. I kicked around a few two by fours and trash that was lying on the floor. I didn't know what I was looking for but I kept rummaging through everything. When I got by the kitchen I saw an envelope sticking out of a pile of ash. It was strange because it looked brand new. I picked it up and there wasn't a burn on it. I opened the letter, and I read:

THE LETTER

Dear Son,

If you ever find this letter, I will probably be long gone from this world now. There are some things I must share with you that you need to know and may disturb you. First of all, you need to know I am your mother Christian and I love you very much. I love you more than anything in this world.

When I was a young girl, I grew up very poor. I never had nice things like new clothes, new shoes or anything like the other kids had. Every day was a struggle for your grandmother and I. Each day I watched her go to work just to make enough money for us to eat once a day. Every night I would go to bed starving because all I had that day was a slice of bread and a cup of water. There were plenty of times we didn't have electricity and we had to make a small fire in the living room to keep warm.

Around the time I was 17, I started to see a man everywhere I went. I'd see him when I left school, I saw him when I went to the store, and I even saw him as I walked out of church at times. He reminded me of a lion, studying his prey until it was the right time to make a move. In the beginning, he never spoke; he'd somehow lock

James Green

eyes with me, I almost felt hypnotized. In the end of the exchange, he'd always give a little smirk. At first, I thought it was creepy, but deep down I began to feel attracted to him. Every day I'd hope to see him again and maybe he would have the courage to speak to me. The day I turned 18 I finally got my wish. I was leaving the local malt shop with some friends one night. I heard someone call my name before I got the chance to cross the street. He was standing by the door waiting for me. I don't know how he knew my name but I didn't take the time to ask. He asked if I minded if he walked me home. I told my friends they could leave and that I would catch up with them the next day. We walked, we talked, and he wanted to know everything about me. Every time I would ask him something about himself, he would just ask me another question about me. I loved to talk so I didn't mind. He was more handsome up close than I ever imagined. He almost seemed to have a glow about himself. His eyes were full of wisdom and he spoke with intelligence. When we finally got to my door he stole my heart with two words... "You're perfect," I remember that as if it were yesterday.

Every day after that, he walked me everywhere I went. He'd already be waiting outside my door when I left in the morning. He loved the morning sun, he once told me the sun was like his father, how beautiful it felt on his back and he would even joke around and say he would worship it if he could. I was intrigued by his poetic way he would speak at times.

James Green

One day he told me he could take me away from the life I was living. There would be no more pain, no more struggling, no more hunger, no more thirst. I was so desperate and in love, I was willing to do anything he wanted me to do. He only asked for one thing in return. He said he wanted the honor of being the father of my first child and that he wanted me to give him a beautiful baby boy. I would soon learn what he meant by the words "give me." Nevertheless, I agreed so he asked me to go to church with him one Sunday. He told me how he loved Sunday and that it was his favorite day of the week. To my surprise, we went to a Catholic church. I met with the priest, he was an old man dressed in a black tunic. They invited me to "Ash Wednesday" where my love told me we would officially start our beginning together.

When that day arrived there was a ceremony, the priest was speaking in Latin as he rubbed black ash on my forehead. When the ceremony was over, I was allowed to go to the bathroom to wash my face. I noticed the cross was longer on the top than it was at the bottom.

My love insisted that we get married the next day. I was nervous but there wasn't anything I wouldn't do for him. We got married the next day and made passionate love that night. It was the most beautiful experience I ever encountered.

James Green

During the next eight months, I experienced things I never thought possible. I lived in a house so huge it could take up a football field. I had all the cars, clothes, jewelry and money anyone could imagine. I must say, during those months I can look back and say I wasn't proud of myself. I forgot where I came from, all the values I'd learned as a young woman were gone and anything my mother taught me had vanished. I began to think I was better than everyone else and people didn't even deserve to walk on the same ground as I did. It was a proud but lonely feeling. I lost all my friends I had growing up; I lost contact with my mother...all I had was the company of your father. You were born that October 31. It was the same day I found out you and your father shared birthdays. I was so drugged up at the hospital your father filled out the birth certificate. Your name was supposed to be Christian Lawrence Smith. When your birth certificate was mailed to us, I noticed your middle name wasn't what I told your father to record. Your certificate read your name to be Christian Lucifer Smith. I hadn't read the Bible but I had been to church numerous times and my mother taught me a few things. There was no way I wanted to name my son after the Devil himself! When I confronted your father about your name, he in a calm manner told me it was time that I give you to him now. He told me that he was taking you and would be leaving forever. There was no way I was going to let that happen. His

James Green

arrogant response was simply, "a deal is a deal." I asked him what deal!

You see my son...all the money, the cars, the house, it all came with a price...and that price was my soul...and you. Your father is a deceiver...a liar; if you ever see him again, please stay away from him! Pray, ask God to protect you and show you the truth. By now, you should know your father's name. His name...is Lucifer.

Even though he is your father in the flesh, he is not your true father. Your one and true father is the father in Heaven, and always remember that. You see in the end I realized and learned a few things. Lucifer loved Sunday so much because he himself placed an unction, authority, and power on Sunday. He deliberately chose the first day of the week as his day because the creator chose the last day of the week to sanctify. He despises the father in Heaven and will go to the ends of the earth to take us away from him. Don't worship on Sunday Christian, no matter who you claim to worship on that day you are paying homage to Lucifer, the Devil. He loved the sun so much because he convinced people ages ago to worship the sun instead of the father in Heaven and considered it a small victory in his plan. He also bore the name "the son of the morning" when he lived in Heaven. Don't consult with the queen of Heaven or the signs of the zodiac. My son those are occult practices, they are traps,

James Green

tricks of Lucifer, and everyone who involves themselves with these things, lives their lives daily with insecurities.

Last but not least, my son, Lucifer does not work alone. He has brothers...demons people call them. Now beware of them, there are three kinds. You have friendly demon spirits; those are the ones that aren't upset about what happened in Heaven. You have warriors; they like to bring destruction to our planet. Lastly you have oppressors, they hate the father in Heaven with every cell in their body and live to terrorize the human race. Now by all means don't be fooled by the friendly demon spirits. They pride themselves in impersonating the dead. Don't be deceived in believing you will be able to contact me after I am gone. Read The Holy Bible my son, no human soul is immortal. Only the chosen ones who give their lives to Christ will live again and live forever!

The human race has been taught to believe in necromancy which is the belief that we all have an immortal soul and that we enter into a higher state of being after we die that was better than the life here on Earth. You don't have to call on any demons for help in this area, all you have to do is believe in life after death and you've already fallen for what Lucifer likes to call...CHRISTIAN IDOLATRY. Son it breaks another commandment as the Sunday worship does and is all in the plan to disqualify us from entering Heaven.

James Green

I love you son and I urge you to seek the truth, don't let Lucifer deceive you as he has done to me. I don't know what he is going to do to me, but I'm sure my time is short; I broke the deal and refused to give you up. And I would break that deal again and again and a million times over. Don't forget me my son, you are special, you always were and you always will be.

Love,

Your Mother

James Green

THE INTERVIEW (part 1)

After reading my mother's letter, I knew then what had to be done. I was tired of the lies, tired of the killing. It was time I faced my father face to face. I didn't know how I was going to do it and I didn't know where. However, I knew that this was the time; there was no doubt in my mind.

I walked out of the burned down house with no destination; by this time it was thundering, the rain was heavy and there was lightning striking everywhere. The rain didn't bother me though, nor did the loud thunder. All I had on my mind was finally facing Lucifer, the Devil himself. I probably walked for an hour before I somehow ended up at the high school. I walked towards the back where the football field was. I knew he had to be somewhere close. There was never a night that he didn't show himself. I stood in the middle of the 50-yard line, massive raindrops were coming down, and the thunder was so loud, the sound of it made my ears hurt, even the lighting was striking nearby, but I had no fear.

I let out a loud cry where I stood, "WHERE ARE YOU. . . I KNOW YOU'RE HERE...LUCIFER!"

I heard the loudest crack of thunder I heard all night. I looked up and saw a light coming down. It seemed so far away at

James Green

first but it began to come down at a rapid pace. As the light came closer, it got brighter and brighter. It was so bright that it became unbearable to look at directly. When the light got about 20 feet above me, I could see it forming into the presence I had been used to seeing my entire life. But this time it was much different. He came down with such grace. I could see every detail about him. His wings were enormous; he had a breastplate encrusted with various stones. His body was cut like a statue of a god like the ones you see in Rome. In addition, his face...his face looked like mine, he had black hair like me. His eyes were red as fire. When he reached the ground, we locked eyes for at least five minutes. The breaths I took were so heavy, it was the first time I faced him with not an ounce of fear in my heart. It didn't look like he was going to say anything anytime soon, so I decided to speak.

CHRISTIAN: so...what shall I call you?

(*His eyes slowly went from blood red to a dark brown, the same color as mine*)

He said in a calm voice...

LUCIFER: *My name is Lucifer, but to you my son, you can call me father.*

CHRISTIAN: *Why have you been following me my whole life, why did you kill all those people?*

James Green

LUCIFER: *Your whole life I have protected you. Anyone that caused you harm, anyone that wanted to take you away from me I destroyed! Like any father would do for his son.*

CHRISTIAN: *But why my mother, why her, why us!*

LUCIFER: *I needed a son. I needed a son to help me lead my army in the battle that is to come. My brothers are soldiers, but they are not leaders, as you are my son. Together we will triumph!*

CHRISTIAN: *Battle? What...battle?*

LUCIFER: *I'm sure you've read of our battle...with them (he looks up).*

CHRISTIAN: *With God?*

LUCIFER: *Of course, but your book is inaccurate, because we will be victorious!*

(He seemed confident in every word he spoke)

CHRISTIAN: *Why should I believe anything you tell me?*

LUCIFER: *(he laughs, raises his chin) Is this an interview?*

James Green

CHRISTIAN: *I read The Holy Bible. I read the letter from my mother, and they say you are a liar, that you are a deceiver! You deceived the angels in Heaven, and you deceived my mother!*

LUCIFER: *Deceived! What do you know about deceit! (a loud thunder sounds; then he points to the sky) He is the deceiver!*

CHRISTIAN: *What did you do Lucifer...what did you do to God?*

LUCIFER: *(he stares at me, I could see the anger in his face; I could see his chest rise with every breath)...I will show you.*

He looks up at the sky, his wings spread as far out as they could. The rain around me stopped. I could still see the rain though. I suddenly felt drowsy like I was falling asleep. I looked at Lucifer with the last drop of energy I had in my body.

CHRISTIAN: *What are you doing to me?*

LUCIFER: *Be calm, open your eyes and see.* I then fell to the ground and fell into a deep sleep.

James Green

THE HEAVENS

I opened my eyes and saw beautiful clouds everywhere; I could see walkways made of gold. Everything was so bright. I walked down one of the golden pathways. I saw angels dressed in white with white wings flying all around me but they didn't seem to notice me. I came upon one of the most beautiful sites I'd ever seen. It reminded me of what I saw on the Internet; it reminded me of what God commanded Moses to build on Earth. I remembered it was supposed to be patterned after the sanctuary in Heaven. There seemed to be one difference though; in all the pictures, I had seen there were always two angels covering the throne or the mercy seat. As I looked upon where the mercy seat was there was only one cherub, one angel covering the glory of God. I looked a little closer...it was Lucifer. The one who sat in the throne was too bright to see. There was a huge rainbow around the throne; and around the throne, there were 24 seats. In each seat sat an old man dressed in white. They all had golden crowns on their heads. There was thunder and lightning and voices but I couldn't understand what they were saying. I could see seven lamps before the throne. There was also a sea of glass that stretched before the throne all the way, to where I stood. There were also for huge beasts around the throne, nothing like I had ever seen before. They all had wings; the first beast looked like a lion, the second looked like a calf, the third had

James Green

the face of a man and the fourth had the face of an eagle. It was amazing, I could never imagine with my own mind such a site. It was as if I wasn't there, no one even noticed me.

Lucifer looked pleased to be in God's presence.

To my surprise, I heard God speak.

> **GOD:** *Lucifer*

The voice was so deep..

> **GOD:** *Gather your brothers, for it is time for worship.*

> **LUCIFER:** *Yes, my Lord.*

When Lucifer flew away the glory and the light he was protecting rested on his back, he looked as bright as the sun. He flew to each section of Heaven gathering the angels. They all seemed to have much respect for him and they obeyed him. Every order I saw God give Lucifer it was carried out the same way, they were like general and colonel, like father and son.

> The next time God sent Lucifer out to gather the angels I heard him speak again, but this time it seemed to be to himself.

> **GOD:** *It is time...the test must be done.*

James Green

I had no idea what was going to happen but the sound of his voice made me tremble. His voice was like thunder.

When Lucifer returned, before he could turn his back to guard the mercy seat, God stopped him, and spoke:

> **GOD:** *Lucifer.*

> **LUCIFER:** *Yes, my Lord.*

> **GOD:** *Thou art the anointed cherub that covereth. I have set thee so. Thou rest upon the Holy mountain of God, thou hast walked up and down in the midst of the stones of fire. I have made thou perfect in every way since the day of your creation. I have covered you with every precious stone.*

> **LUCIFER:** *Yes, my Lord.*

> **GOD:** *The time has come; it is time to anoint once again an angel of Heaven. He will rule Heaven by my side. To what I ask you shall I grant him? I will let thou think to thyself then bring back an answer.*

> **LUCIFER:** *Yes, my Lord.*

Lucifer flew away to a place where he could be alone and think to himself. He paced back and forth. For a short while, he seemed confused, and then, it seemed like he had an epiphany.

James Green

LUCIFER: *The Lord must be referring to me! I am the closest to being like the father; the angelic host already obeys my every command. He is going to make me a king! And a king...deserves worship!*

He flew back to God with his great idea in mind. He didn't want to seem prideful so he remained humble, believing that God was referring to him.

GOD: *Lucifer, does thou hast an answer?*

LUCIFER: Yes, my Lord. I suggest your anointed one receive worship.

GOD: *Worship? I am God! Leave me!*

Lucifer flies back to think about what he said. He wonders if he should've kept his idea to himself. He didn't know whether to stay or go back. He rests until he hears his name called throughout the Heavens.

GOD: *LUCIFER*

Lucifer quickly returns to God.

LUCIFER: *Yes, my Lord.*

James Green

GOD: *I have considered your suggestion; the anointed one shall receive worship! Gather all your brothers and I shall announce it to all the Heavens.*

LUCIFER: *Yes, my Lord!*

With a huge smile on his face he begin to fly away.

GOD: *Lucifer, I will need another covering cherub while thou gather the angels, bring Michael so that he may cover the mercy seat.*

LUCIFER: *Yes, my Lord, it shall be done.*

He flies away and fetches Michael the angel. There is nothing special about Michael; he was an average angel, with no special duties that set him apart from any other angel. He wasn't covered with precious stones as Lucifer was; he was quiet, humble.

LUCIFER: *Michael.*

MICHAEL: *Yes, Lucifer.*

LUCIFER: *The Lord has called thee to guard the mercy seat. It is of great privilege and great honor to do so.*

MICHAEL: *Yes, Lucifer. But art thou the covering cherub?*

James Green

LUCIFER: *Yes, of course, but I may not be for much longer, now go!*

MICHAEL: *Yes, Lucifer.*

Michael obeyed as all the angelic host did to Lucifer. He flew to where God resided and without word or question, spread his wings and covered the mercy seat.

In the meantime, Lucifer gathered all the angels of Heaven. He was so excited about the announcement that was soon to come but he didn't speak a word to anyone about what the gathering was going to be about.

It had taken about an hour for all the angels to gather in one place for the ceremony. There were thousands upon thousands of angels gathered. There were too many to count. As far as they eye could see you could see them all, standing in line, waiting for the Lord to speak.

When Lucifer returned to the throne, he and Michael stood in front of the mercy seat equal distance apart. Michael stood to the right of the seat; he had his left wing spread, Lucifer stood to the left and had his right wing spread. It seemed as if the glory and light had to always be covered. Lucifer blew a trumpet to get the attention of all the angels. There was a silence in Heaven for at least 30 minutes.

James Green

Everyone stood at attention, there was discipline among them. After 30 minutes exactly, God spoke.

> **GOD:** *My children, I have gathered thee here to honor and glorify our new and anointed one. He shall receive worship as I. He will rule the Heavens side by side with me. He will be one with me, a God...my son.*

I could see Lucifer's chin raised. He had a small grin on his face. He was patiently waiting for his moment he had been yearning for.

> **GOD:** *My children...I hereby proclaim...*

Lucifer lifts his left foot as he was going to take a step forward.

> **GOD:** *Michael! He shall be the anointed one, you shall worship him as you've worshipped me. He will rule the Heavens side by side, with the Father.*

You could see Lucifer's face almost melt. *Michael?* he said to himself. The entire angelic host took a knee to give worship to the newly anointed one. They all were on one knee...except Lucifer.

> **GOD:** *Lucifer, bow to the king of Heaven as thine hast asked of you.*

He stared at Michael with a deep, dark look on his face. Then he took a bow.

James Green

LUCIFER: *Yes, my Lord.*

I could see the anger on his face as he stared at the ground. A tear rolled down his cheek.

They all worshiped Michael. They were all on one knee "holy, holy, holy, Lord God Almighty, which was, and is, and is to come. Thou art worthy O' Lord to receive glory and honor and power, for thou hast created all things, and for thy pleasure they are and were created," I could hear them say. And they all gave glory to Michael.

When worship was over, the two cherubs Michael and Lucifer returned to their positions, facing each other on the mercy seat. Soon Lucifer's tears stopped, but you could see the empty look on his face. I thought he was going to ask God why he chose Michael instead of him. Instead, he said nothing. After a short while Lucifer spoke.

LUCIFER: *My Lord.*

GOD: *Yes, Lucifer.*

LUCIFER: *May I be excused from the throne for a short while, my Lord?*

GOD: *Yes Lucifer, Michael will guard the mercy seat while thou are away.*

James Green

LUCIFER: *Thank you My Lord.*

I thought Lucifer was going to fly to his place where he could be alone and think. Instead, I saw him flying all over Heaven, talking to all the angels. To my surprise, he seemed to be accusing God of unfair treatment to him and the entire angelic host. He told them that they were as slaves and had no free will and that they were as animals that could only obey what they were told. He accused Michael for going behind everyone's back in Heaven making them look bad so that he could be chosen by God. And he did this for what looked like days.

Back at the throne, Michael heard God let out a sigh.

MICHAEL: *Is everything ok, My Lord?*

GOD: *YES, MICHAEL.*

It seemed like another few days went by, then God spoke to Michael again.

GOD: *MICHAEL*

MICHAEL: *Yes, my Lord.*

GOD: *Bring Lucifer that I may speak with him.*

MICHAEL: *Yes, my Lord, it shall be done.*

James Green

Michael flew throughout Heaven in search for Lucifer. He found him among a group of angels; they were all gathered around him in a circle, listening to him speak. He seemed to be speaking with much emotion. Michael couldn't hear what was being said, but his job was to obey what God had told him to do, so he called out to Lucifer.

MICHAEL: *Lucifer.*

He called out to Lucifer amongst the angels. He turned around slowly, knowing who it was that called his name.

LUCIFER: *What?*

MICHAEL: *The father wishes to speak with you.*

And they both flew back to the throne Lucifer behind Michael. The eyes of Lucifer looked as if he wanted to harm Michael, but he didn't.

Michael returned to his position in front of the mercy seat as Lucifer stood in front, then took a knee.

LUCIFER: *You called for me, my Lord.*

GOD: *I have Lucifer, will thou gather all the angels of Heaven so that I may speak to them?*

Lucifer looked confused wondering why God didn't have Michael complete the task instead of calling him back just to go back out to do it.

James Green

LUCIFER: *It shall be done.*

With pride in his heart, he took his time gathering the angelic host. After a few hours or so, they were all gathered before the throne. There was no order to the gathering, no lines as there were before. Lucifer stood in front of the mass, with about half the angelic host standing behind him. The other half seemed to be separated. And God spoke...

GOD: *LUCIFER.*

Lucifer didn't kneel, but responded

LUCIFER: *Yes, my Lord.*

GOD: *Thou hast sinned; thou art the accuser of the brethren, why hast thou done so?*

Lucifer stood proud, but didn't utter a word.

GOD: *Michael, please stand before thy brothers of Heaven.*

Michael gets up from his position and stands before the throne facing the Heavens. And God spoke again...

GOD: *Behold, Michael, the archangel, and the son of God. He is me, and I am him. To have served him, you have served me. He wasn't created as I have created you. He is the living test, the proof of love and loyalty. I know of who*

James Green

have joined your brother Lucifer in false accusing my son. This is your time, you shall worship, and I shall forgive.

And all the angels looked around at each other with fear and surprise. Lucifer's eyes were as big as saucers. I could tell he felt the mistake he made. Why didn't he just obey God? He was the closest thing to God. Anything he wanted would have been given to him if he had just been loyal and obeyed. I could see now that pride was the beginning of Lucifer's downfall.

GOD: *Lucifer, you shall bow to my son, without anger and envy but with love and loyalty and thou shall be forgiven.*

Lucifer stood there with his chest out, I could see more pride building. He looked behind him. A third of the angelic host stood behind him as if they were on his side. The other two thirds were in line and kneeling to Michael, praising him. With his loyal followers, there was no turning back now. He looked at Michael with disgust, and then turned to the throne. And he spoke...

LUCIFER: *I shall not bow! I will exalt my throne above the stars of you! I will sit upon the mount of the congregation, in the sides of the north. I will ascend above the heights of the clouds, I will be...as the most high!*

In the blink of an eye the throne began to be surrounded by fire, it seemed as it were building up and about to explode. All the

James Green

angels turned their backs because the force was so bright, they all knew Lucifer was going to be destroyed that instant. The fire grew larger and larger, then instantly, I heard the sound of thunder and a flash of bright light. I was blinded so I couldn't see what happened.

When the light died down, everyone turned to look. They all, including I expected to see Lucifer destroyed. But to a surprise, we saw Michael, covering Lucifer with his wing. He had saved Lucifer from being eradicated by God. Lucifer opened his eyes; he looked around, patted himself and noticed he was still alive. He let out a loud and evil laugh. His followers did as he did, they all laughed with Lucifer. And Lucifer spoke...

LUCIFER: *Thou art weak, thou dost not deserve to sit upon the throne!*

Simultaneously I could see God's thoughts and I saw something happen to Lucifer. I saw God thinking that if he destroyed Lucifer, then the rest of the angelic host would serve out of fear instead of love. God was love and didn't want to see that happen. The same time darkness fell upon Lucifer and his followers. They all became black figures. And God spoke...

GOD: *Michael.*

Michael turned to God, wondering if what he had done was wrong.

James Green

GOD: *Lucifer the accuser is now Satan, the devil, he shall not dwell in the Heavens.... attack!*

And there was a war in Heaven. Michael and his angels fought against Lucifer and his angels. Lucifer and the one third of the angels that followed him didn't prevail; they were cast out of Heaven and fell to earth. And as quick as they were cast out, I fell to Earth with them. Then I woke up...

I was still a little drowsy, but that moment felt like the first clear moment I had experienced in my life. As I began to fathom what just happened, the questions began to form....

James Green

THE INTERVIEW (part 2)

LUCIFER: *Now do you see, I was treated unfairly and I shall have my revenge. My soldiers are trained and with you by my side, we will not lose again.*

CHRISTIAN: *Why me Lucifer, I'm not an angel, what could I possibly offer you?*

LUCIFER: *You are the key my son, the son of God shall face the son of the dragon. You are prophecy fulfilled. You shall serve as the Anti-christ!*

CHRISTIAN: *Anti-Christ?*

LUCIFER: *Don't worry, much is rewarded to whom serves me, I am fair, I am here! I give to who worship me whatever he desires! I don't lead from afar and treat others unfairly. I will give you...your Amy back. I will give you all the riches your mind can imagine...all these things will I give thee...if thou wilt fall down and worship me!*

Right then my life seemed to flash before my eyes. I thought about my mother and her words, I thought about Amy. I thought about what Lucifer had done to her. I thought about all the

James Green

times God tried to show me the truth but I ignored him. I knew it was God who was truly keeping me alive so that I could see the truth. I saw that God wasn't unfair; he only required loyalty and love. I reached for my book bag where I kept my Bible but it wasn't there. I was scared; I didn't know what to do, so I fell to my knees...

> **LUCIFER:** *Yes my son, you have made the right choice.*

I fell to my knees, but not to worship Lucifer, I fell to my knees and began to say the Lord's Prayer.

> **CHRISTIAN:** *Our father, which art in Heaven, hallowed be thy name, they kingdom come...*

Lucifer began to be surrounded by fire.

> **LUCIFER:** *What are you doing?!*

Lightning struck, I was scared, but I kept going.

> **CHRISTIAN:** *...thy will be done in earth, as it is in Heaven. Give us this day our daily bread...*

And more lightening struck and thunder sounded, Lucifer became enraged!

> **LUCIFER:** *Do you know what you are doing! You will regret the words you spew from your mouth!*

rew around him, and began to burn him; he began to scream in agony

> **LUCIFER:** *Nooooooooooo, you shall die.... Christian!*

I finished my prayer.

> **CHRISTIAN:** *and forgive us our debts, as we forgive our debtors. And lead us not into temptation, but deliver us from evil, for thine is the kingdom, and the power, and the glory! Forever! Amen!*

And before Lucifer could stretch his arm out of the fire to grab me, the sky opened! A figure too bright grabbed the ball of flame that held Lucifer and drove it under ground. When I noticed the light wasn't as bright I turned to look up, I could only see the crack in the sky. Then a voice spoke...

> **VOICE:** *I AM PLEASED, THOU ART FORGIVEN.*

The sky closed, I looked around, and the rain had stopped. I laughed as an insane person would, because I knew no one would believe what I just heard or saw. I turned and took a step to leave, and I fell to the ground.

James Green

THE REALIZATION

When I woke up, I wasn't in the middle of the football field anymore. It seemed like it was only a second ago. I was sitting at a desk back at school. I looked down and all my clothes were white, my shirt, my pants, my socks, my shoes, even my book bag. I looked up and saw my English teacher Ms. Kirkpatrick teaching a lesson she had already taught us. I looked around at all the students; everyone was paying attention to the chalkboard where the lesson was being taught. I looked behind me and my heart dropped. It was Amy; it looked like she was trying to finish some homework she hadn't completed before the teacher came and collected it. The moment seemed so familiar. She looked up at me, gave me a little grin and went back to work.

I looked to the chair next to Amy where Brad usually sat but he wasn't there. Suddenly a balled up piece of notebook paper hit me in the back of the head. I turned around and realized it was Brad; he was sitting a few rows in front of me instead of the chair I remember him sitting in. I then realized something even more unbelievable; I had this intense feeling of déjà vu. I quickly reached for my cell phone. When I opened it I couldn't believe my eyes. The first thing I saw was a text message from Mark reminding me we were supposed to grab something to eat after I got out of school. What

was even more strange was the date on the phone. The date was 12 months ago; it was the first week of school. But wait, 12 months ago? I didn't remember knowing Mark then. I opened my book bag expecting to see my Satanic Bibel but saw the book I began to read that very day 12 months ago...The Holy Bible.

The bell rang and everyone was dismissed from class. As I walked to my locker, I bumped shoulders with someone. I looked up to apologize and I saw that it was the strange girl with the nice glasses. She had on the same white shirt and jeans as before. She had the biggest smile on her face, "Hello Christian," she said. There was a short pause, I was still a little confused, and she was still smiling. "Aren't you going to ask me about wanting to know the truth or something?" I asked her. She laughed, "No"; she gave me a hug before she walked away, "You already know the truth." As she walked away, no one saw her or acknowledged her. I turned around to head to my locker, then I remembered I never knew the girl's name. "Hey," I shouted, I quickly ran back down the hall to find her but she was gone, it was as if she just disappeared.

On my way back to my locker, I saw Amy and Brad talking to each other. Brad had on his varsity jacket and Amy was holding her books just as I remembered. I started grinning because I knew this was the part where we were supposed to lock eyes. When our eyes locked my small grin became a big goofy one. I got so excited I forgot what

James Green

was supposed to happen next. I suddenly remembered as my head was headed towards the lockers after a sucker punch from Brad. I wasn't unconscious but my eyes were closed. I knew how the rest of the story was supposed to go. I felt a familiar gust of wind. I took a deep breath, I was ready to get up and face Lucifer again. As I was helped up I turned around and it was Amy. The hallway wasn't empty this time. People were standing around looking at me, security was taking Brad away, and someone closed the outside door in the hallway where the wind was coming from. "I'm sorry about that," Amy said as she fixed my hair and clothes. "He's such a jerk...I'm Amy by the way." It was a little strange listening to her introduce herself after all we had been through. Instead of telling her some crazy story that would've run her away after the first 30 seconds I just smiled and introduced myself, "Christian."

As I walked away, thinking of the past year and this obsession, I realized that it cost me everything. It cost me my girlfriend, the life of my best friend and even my sanity, but God allowed me to gain it all back. For the first time in my life I felt complete. I was happy; I had another chance with Amy, Mark was alive, I even had the courage to make new friends...and most importantly my life wasn't a mystery anymore. I knew who I was, I knew who my mother was and I knew that she loved me. Most importantly I finally knew who my father was... my real father.

James Green

THE END

James Green

ABOUT THE AUTHOR

Darek James Green was born February 17, 1982. He grew up in Warrensville Heights, a suburb of Cleveland Ohio. He is the son of Willie James Green and Joyce Green. He has a son Dillan James Green born February 10, 2010. He has two older sisters Crystal Kelly (daughter of Joyce Green) and Kawanis Hobson (daughter of Willie Green) but for the most part grew up as an only child. He was shy as a kid. Kids usually teased him about being overweight.

As a child he liked to draw. It was a way to take his mind off the other kids and also gain approval at the same time. After a dramatic weight loss after the fifth grade Darek stopped drawing and turned his focus towards school work and hanging out with friends. He graduated with a 2. 9 GPA from Warrensville Heights high school. That same summer he enlisted in the United States Army where he would spend the next four years. Within that time he was married for 18 months to a young woman he went to high school with. When he returned home from duty he served another four years in the Army Reserve while attending college. He went to Cuyahoga Community College then transferred to ITT Technical Institute where he would obtain an Associate's degree in Computer Networking Systems. After graduation Darek became a real estate

James Green

investor, he bought a few houses and rented them to tenants throughout the city of Cleveland. When the market crashed he became a small concert and party promoter, promoting parties and small concerts in Alabama and Georgia. After a tough loss Darek sold his home and moved to Beachwood Ohio where he started his own cleaning franchise.

Throughout his life Darek always believed in God but it was strictly based on faith. He one day wanted to know more and why he should believe in what he believed in. He was led to a video he saw on Youtube about music and how it was related to Satanism. That intrigued him to want to know even more, so he began to read The Holy Bible and even listen to testimonies from ex Satanists. After a year or so of research Darek found a church he could call home at Southeast 7th day Adventist church in Cleveland Ohio. There was still a void that needed to be filled. Darek wanted to help spread the word of God but was never a good speaker and was too shy to talk in front of a group of people. After research and prayer he finally decided to write a book. He would use his creative side and combine some of the research he has done for the last two years; And here we are now...with **LUCIFER:** THE INTERVIEW

James Green

A SPECIAL THANK YOU TO:

I would like to give special thanks the following people. You were all a substantial influences to make my book come together.

- Jesus Christ
- Joyce Green
- Willie Green
- Ashley Hill
- Christopher Hudson
- Roger Morneau
- Jonnetta Macon
- Wendy Peterson
- DeVaughn Lilly
- Crystal Kelly
- Pedro Romera
- Pastor Jerome Hurst
- Dr. Eric Dwight Haynes
- Digital Daggers
- Lykke Li
- Adele
- Enya

Made in the USA
Charleston, SC
21 May 2012